SWIMMING IN CIRCLES

Fanny Frewen

The Book Guild Ltd
Sussex, England

First published in Great Britain in 2002 by
The Book Guild Ltd
25 High Street,
Lewes, East Sussex
BN7 2LU

Typesetting in Baskerville by
Keyboard Services, Luton, Bedfordshire

Printed in Great Britain by
Antony Rowe Ltd, Chippenham, Wiltshire

A catalogue record for this book is available from
The British Library

ISBN 1 85776 691 1

1

I stood by helplessly as I watched Jenny falling in love.

Jenny was not my grandchild. She was no relation of mine at all. She was not my responsibility, she was my friend. I had known her since she was a schoolgirl. She first came my way because she was looking for a job to do in the holidays to earn some pocket money. 'Could I do some weeding?' she asked. I was hesitant at first, having been had that way before, to the detriment of our flower borders. But I had taken to Jenny because she spoke clearly, in a pleasant voice, so I took a chance. Luckily, she did know weed from seedling.

My husband loved the strimmer and the sit-on mower. On the latter, he was a positive lawn-lout, you could hear him doing wheelies from the other side of the house, but he has always reckoned that real men don't do weeding.

Jenny's mother and father were a couple I would scarcely have bothered to get to know if it hadn't been for my increasing affection for their daughter. Her father, a retired colonel, was on the parish council and so right-wing he made me look like a Marxist. His name was Bill and his wife was called Margaret.

Bill and Margaret Patterson. I thought of them in that order as Bill was very much the master of the house. I had thought that the expression 'My husband would never allow me to do that ... wear that ... smoke ... drink spirits,' was gone for good. But, in the case of the Pattersons, it was not.

Jenny's older sister was, by that time, married to an army officer, a nice dull man who was in their father's regiment. She was pretty but, in my opinion, Jenny was beautiful, with large dark blue eyes and eyelashes you could hang the washing on, rather wide cheekbones and a chin which, though not small, was a good shape. She was quite bosomy but had narrow hips and good legs.

There were photographs of Sally's wedding in the Pattersons' sitting room, a room where I dared not light a cigarette. We were not present on that occasion, which was just as well as Charlie, my own husband, would have looked a good deal more elegant in a morning suit than Bill Patterson had. As Mr Pooter would have said, he seemed rather short for an officer. But there was the picture, recording for all time the bride in white, carrying lilies that looked as though they ought to be put in the freezer to await the funeral, the parents, the in-laws, and Jenny as bridesmaid in a shade of blue that did not suit her. 'With her blue eyes we thought *blue*,' I can hear Margaret saying. What a pity Bill hadn't used his prerogative to say, 'But not that blue.'

When Jenny left school, she wanted to go to university, but Bill and, of course, Margaret, had no intention of allowing their remaining girl to leave home. Jenny was made to attend a secretarial college, going up to London on the train every day and returning every evening. To relieve her feelings, she would come over to our place and dig in the garden. I heard her crashing the fork into a clod of dry earth and yelling, 'Computer skills' in a voice that sounded more as though she was yelling, 'Bugger it.' I sympathised. I was a quill pen person myself.

Once the hated skills were accomplished, Jenny was put into a job by her father, working for a friend of his in an estate agent's. She was allowed to learn to drive, as Bill did consider driving to be a suitable female accomplishment. I'm pretty sure that the only reason Margaret had been allowed a car was in order to drive Bill home from parties. Jenny's little car, very much second-hand, was not only the joy of her life but it also represented her only freedom.

It was in our house that she first met Peter Baker.

Peter had, over the years, become a great friend of ours. He was forty years old, extremely talented, divorced, and had been born in a council house in Balham. At the start of his career, he was my junior. He was eminently fanciable. Although I was at least twenty years older than him, and already even then long and happily married to Charlie, one of the best parts of my job was having, from time to time, lunch with Peter. He had a great deal to learn, but he enjoyed learning it as much as I enjoyed teaching it.

My friendship with Peter served only to enhance my marriage, and Charlie relished the results. When you have been married for several years, interest can flag. I do think it is a pity that office flirtations are now indictable as harassment. They were, in my opinion, marriage savers. Thanks to Peter's admiration, I felt myself to be a much more exciting woman and Charlie reaped the benefit and responded to it with enthusiasm.

Quite soon, I was able to get Peter a substantial rise in salary. He was delighted with himself. 'I'm paying for lunch today, Annie. I can afford it,' he would say. But, like so many miracle-drugs, his well-earned bounty had a side effect. He got married.

His wife's name was Maria and she was by birth Italian. Her father had a little grocery and vegetable shop and he and her mother were delighted that she was marrying a well-off young man. Maria was not just Italian by birth but a real Italian wife. She wanted babies. She wanted Peter to invest his new-found wealth in business with her father.

Papa, a delightfully idle fellow who stuffed himself with his own pasta, already had grandchildren and wanted more. He had turned sitting in a chair with a grandchild on his lap into an art form.

I met Peter's father-in-law at the wedding and liked him, but I did fear for Peter. Maria was got up to the nines for the wedding, which (Catholic of course, although Peter was not a Catholic) was overtly a jolly occasion with a lot of dancing and a great deal of wine. Peter was very drunk by the end of it but managed, bossed about by Maria, to sharpen his wits in time to catch the 'plane which was to take them to Naples.

I only learnt later that, for Maria, contraception was out of the question. In her view, honeymoon conception was the matter in hand. Having been kept at arm's length until after the wedding, Peter told me, 'I certainly didn't want to start a baby at that point. For God's sake, I hadn't even been allowed a bonk so far. And once I was engaged to Maria, I was a good boy and I kept away from other girls. And she did have a lovely body, sort of pale beige, and a most enticing bum, irresistible. I lived in dread for months.' However, somehow it seemed that nature was on Peter's side, and no baby appeared.

Maria, I found out, was very like her mother, an expert in capitalising the nominally subservient role. I didn't dislike her, but I was not in the least sorry for her. She had far prettier and more expensive clothes than she would otherwise have had. She refused to move into the Thames-side flat Peter hankered after and insisted upon a detached house in Bromley, just down the line from her family. 'I'd already grown up in poor suburbia,' said Peter, 'and I loathed the prospect of middle class suburbia. But I did it, like a fool, and I hated it and I was always getting home later and later, as you knew at the time.'

He had difficulty getting his divorce. In the end it was

granted on the grounds that Maria's childlessness could qualify for an annulment. Peter despised the hypocrisy for, of course, the marriage had been consummated. 'But I would have done anything to get out of the mess, and by that time poor Maria wanted it too. It wasn't her fault, poor girl, but mine for being too stupid to realise what it meant to marry into an Italian family. I was glad when she married again and got her babies.'

I stayed friends with Peter, even after I gave up my job to move with Charlie to the country. We could afford to do it in modest comfort, having both worked hard enough to have some money we could live on. Once I got used to the drastic change in my way of life, from highly paid and considerably travelled advertising woman to country wife, I began to enjoy it.

Jenny was fascinated by Peter from the first moment she set eyes on him. I had asked her over to supper while he was with us for a weekend merely because I liked her and I thought the sight of so pretty a girl would be fun for Peter. I was sure he would like her but if I had known what was to happen, I would have invited the local merry widow sooner.

2

I only slowly got to know Jenny Patterson's family.

Jenny went to school with other girls from a more or less similar background to her own. Her older sister, Sally, had been a boarder but Jenny was a day girl. The school was only about thirteen miles from Littlefold and it was decreed that she could perfectly easily get there and back by bus.

She would have liked to be a boarder. According to Sally, boarders had a lot more fun. But when her father announced his decision that Jenny was to go to school by day, her mother's happiness at the prospect buoyed her up. 'Darling, I hope you don't mind being a day girl, but Daddy knows how dreadfully I would miss you.'

'Didn't you miss Sally?'

'Of course I did.' Jenny knew this was not entirely true.

Homecroft, although a private school, was a great deal less expensive than Roedean, Benenden or Cheltenham. A friend of Jenny's, a cynical girl with the unlikely name of Loveday, observed at lunch on one occasion, 'Cat stew. Well, with two brothers at Eton, that's one's lot. Cheap and cheerless.'

Although she was never told in so many words that Sally was Daddy's favourite, Jenny could not help but find it out, and that she, Jenny, was a disappointment for not having been born a boy, a shortcoming she tried to rectify by her behaviour even as a small child.

Sally had long wavy hair which Colonel Patterson would

stroke lovingly, but Jenny believed her only chance of gaining her father's affection was to be as like a boy as possible. She cut off her own hair with her mother's nail scissors. She stomped about the garden dragging her father's heavy cricket bat behind her. She fell out of trees and refused to cry, however much it hurt.

Sally yelled her head off at a nettle sting and was comforted by her father. Jenny began to understand that she did not please him, but she continued to try. She did not seek her mother's approbation. Only very slowly did she become aware at all of that gentle, ineffectual woman.

Everyone at school hated their parents. 'Well,' said one, 'I don't actually *hate* them, but they are so dim. I mean, like, they don't know about anything. They don't know the world.'

'I told them my mother did,' said Jenny.

Her father, Colonel Patterson, had bought the house in Littlefold before he actually retired from the Army, but it had been the family home from day one. Obviously, Littlefold represented everything he held most dear. The High Street was flanked by picturesque old houses, each with its charming garden; a mahonia, a rhododendron and a rambler rose in the front, a long lawn, flower borders and a vegetable garden behind. The Church towered over all, and the relics of Admirals and Generals tottered about with the ancient dogs they'd acquired from rescue kennels, and collected their Daily Telegraphs from the shop.

Better still, Littlefold was outskirted by council houses, from which Colonel Patterson acquired a gardener-handyman for himself and a 'char', as he always called women who clean house, for his wife. As far as I could make out, none of them ever stayed very long with the Pattersons, and Margaret very often did the cleaning herself.

I knew Margaret Patterson as a sad but uncomplaining woman. Only once did she say anything to Jenny, the

7

latter once told me, that caused her to believe that she was anything less than content with life at Littlefold. They had gone to London for the day, largely to get a school uniform for Jenny, at Peter Jones. Wandering about the shop, Jenny saw the restaurant and said, 'Can we have lunch here, Mummy?'

'Oh no, better not. It would be far too expensive. We'll go to a pub and have a sandwich. That'll be just as nice, and I'll let you have a glass of wine. Only don't tell Daddy, he wouldn't approve.' Her mother smiled as they made their way to the pub. 'I love this part of London. I'd always dreamt of living in Chelsea some day.'

'Does Daddy know that?'

'Goodness me, no. He loves it at Littlefold. I wouldn't dream of upsetting him. Anyway, we couldn't possibly have afforded to live anywhere round here. These houses cost millions.'

Catching the train to go home, Jenny had looked longingly at the First Class carriages. She had only been in a First Class carriage once in her life, and that was because she was going up to London with her father, to be handed over to an aunt with whom she was to stay for a few days. He, naturally, always travelled First, because he was an officer and the army paid the fare.

Neither Jenny nor her mother were fat but even so they were uncomfortably crushed into the too-small, over-crowded seat in their part of the train. It was impossible to read, impossible to talk. So Jenny sat thinking. The expensive new uniform (Jenny had outgrown the first set) was above her head in the rack. New blazer, new coat, new skirt and blouses, all stowed in their lovely Peter Jones bags. Once they were fairly in the school uniform department, her mother had taken on a sort of reckless-ness, signing the account slips with an abandon that surprised Jenny.

She began to feel a bit guilty about how much all this had cost. And that was when she resolved to get a holiday job, and why she eventually came to ask me if she could work in our garden.

This was how I began to become fond of her. I was surprised and delighted when she took a liking to me. I could see no reason for a pretty young girl to take an interest in a rather scruffy ageing woman. The days of smart dressing are, for me, long gone by.

Our home was once a farmhouse, situated about half a mile outside the village. Because it was big (it was a substantial farm and was added to by the owners before us) with a nice garden and a sizeable pond, it looked grander than it really was. I found myself to be a hopeless housewife. Having spent many years of my life sufficiently gainfully employed to be able to have a reliable daily help, I had never learnt to do housework, and had no wish to find out at this late stage how it was done. Any efforts I did make were given to the garden, and if Rita, my help, didn't turn up for her once-a-week do-around, it just got neglected unless Charlie took the hoover in hand.

We had a reputation for being stand-offish. We didn't intend to be, but that's apparently how it seemed. I suppose it was for that reason that Colonel Patterson wanted to get to know us.

During the summer holiday when Jenny was working in our garden, I found myself seated next to Bill Patterson at a dinner party with people who had been kind enough to continue asking us so many times that we really had to go. He was very jovial. 'I hope my girl is earning her wages,' he said. 'I hear you are a keen gardener.'

'It's more, really, that I have a keen garden,' I replied.

'Have you lived here long?' he went on.

'A few years. We love the place.' This was what I always

said. It was true, in its way, and I did want to seem friendly.

'So do we. Tell me, Mrs Finlay, what did your husband do?'

'He was managing director of an advertising agency.' I had by now long given up expecting to be asked what, if anything, I had ever done myself. I had once made the mistake of answering the question about my husband and facetiously adding, 'and if you'd like to know what I did, I was a prostitute until my legs gave out.' The laugh that followed was more one of embarrassment than mirth.

One of my great luxuries was our swimming pool. My excuse for having it put in at first was Charlie's dodgy back. He took a bad fall on manoeuvres when he was doing his National Service. When it hurt him, he did a lot of groaning and required a lot of massage from me. But he hardly ever went into the pool. He said cold water would permanently atrophy the muscles. The pool wasn't cold. It was in the remotest but also the sunniest part of the garden, so although we didn't heat it, it was gloriously warm all summer and well into the autumn. But Charlie didn't believe me so I usually had it to myself, or I did until I invited Jenny to use it whenever she wanted. The invitation was a sop to my conscience but Jenny's pleasure was a joy. It was delightful to see her, as naked and as unself-conscious as a fish, swimming happily about.

'Mrs Finlay is so kind, Daddy. You know she lets me swim in her lovely pool.'

'A swimming pool!' said Bill Patterson. 'It's all right for some. I suppose you made a packet, selling soap. A bit different from us old soldiers.' I could see he was turning nasty on his third glass of claret.

'But you served your country, don't forget that,' said his wife on cue, placatingly.

So had Charlie served his country. But *I* knew how to put away a few tumblers and still mind my manners.

I was absolutely certain that I was the only person to be told when Jenny lost her virginity. I had known her for some time by then. It was before her sister Sally was married, although she was engaged, and had a solitaire diamond set in a platinum ring to prove it. Ever her father's girl, she was 'old-fashioned' to a tiresome degree. I hoped (although I didn't much care) that the wedding night would go off all right. Sally, I guessed, was a latter-day Maria, who hadn't allowed my friend Peter to so much as unfasten her bra before the knot was tied.

I knew Jenny loathed her job at the estate agent's. If only she had been allowed to pursue the career she had wanted, how different things might have been. As it was, the nearest she ever came to being an architect was being violated by one.

I was aware that she kept her end up in her tedious capacity by adopting a blasé air. She was usually simple and sweet with me, but even I had noticed it. Her working day would have driven me mad. I never minded running errands and making the tea, as I had had to do when I was a cub copywriter. But the endless boredom of transcribing ponderous, pompous letters, their illiteracy scarcely disguised by the use of five words where one apt one would suffice, would have sent me straight into the arms of any passing lorry driver.

'I suppose it was partly my own fault,' she said pathetically. 'He thought I knew more than I did, you see.' I did, indeed, see the effect that Jenny's pretence of sophistication must have had on the young man. 'We'd been out for a drink after work once or twice. I hadn't met many men, even Sally's husband's best man was quite old and married. So it did seem quite nice.'

'Did you think you were falling in love?' I asked.

'Not really. I would have liked to think so, but no, I wasn't. I couldn't think of anything to say when we were out, but that didn't matter, he talked about himself mostly. I did tell him I envied him being an architect because it was what I had wanted to be.'

'What did he say to that?' I asked.

'He said that clambering over buildings in all weathers was men's work and why would a pretty girl like me want to ruin her looks that way?'

'Oh my goodness, they don't still talk that sort of rubbish, do they?' I asked. 'I thought at least things had changed that far.' It seems that one evening, over a drink, the young man had asked Jenny if she was on the pill. So I asked if she had told him she was actually a virgin.

'No I didn't. I didn't want him to think no one else had ever fancied me. Anyway, then he disappeared into the gents.'

'Thank God for that,' I thought.

It wasn't easy to get the squalid details out of Jenny. For one thing, I didn't want to embarrass her. I was, after all, still 'Mrs Finlay' to her at that point. But I did manage to piece together what had happened.

Jenny has never been overly self-assured, and at that time she clearly had no awareness of her own sex appeal. No doubt she allowed the young man to kiss her, a liberty which was obviously interpreted as leading him on. It seems they were walking across the churchyard at the time.

Looking a long way back, my own first experience of sex had been, to say the most of it, boring and unrewarding. But at least I hadn't been tipped over backwards and violently deflowered on an ancient grave. I was very touched that Jenny should take me this far into her confidence, though not in the least surprised that the unpleasant event had not been reported at home.

3

I learnt from Jenny that the young architect, now that she wanted no more to do with him, had taken up with a girl in the office called Beverley. 'I'm not much cop at secretarial skills myself,' she said, 'but Beverley's a lot worse. Her spelling's so atrocious she can't even look up a word on the Spellcheck.' She laughed but it was clear that her self-confidence had suffered a bad blow.

It would have been much better for her if she could have got clear away from Littlefold. But there was no possibility of that. Her home life, while stultifying, was at least secure. She was underpaid at the estate agent's and had no belief in her ability to earn enough elsewhere to live on. She was also, I knew, worried about her mother, who was not very well.

Margaret Patterson never admitted to feeling unwell, but Jenny noticed a gradual change in her. She seemed sometimes to be overwhelmed with lethargy. She was observant of her, having come to love her very much, largely in response to the love that she had always received in that quarter.

Her sister Sally was now very much the married woman, with a baby son, the apple (whatever that may mean) of his grandfather's eye.

Colonel Patterson had transferred his power base from the officers' mess to the family home. That she was uneasy in her father's presence never struck Jenny as being anyone's fault but her own. Everyone at school had claimed that their parents were old-fashioned, so the situation in which she found herself must obviously be normal.

She usually got home at about half past five. Her boss, approaching retirement, did not work long hours. Jenny, arriving home, would often find that her mother had gone to her room but that her father was busy.

He had set up a tapestry frame upon which he proceeded to embroider his Regimental emblem. In addition to this, he took up cooking, making red-hot curries that took a minimum of five pans for Margaret to scour out afterwards. He mended the vacuum cleaner, which blew up in defiance. He was around the house morning, noon and night, for breakfast, for coffee, for lunch and for dinner. Margaret had suggested he get a dog but he didn't like dogs. Jenny ironed the table-napkins. It was the best thing she could think of to do for her mother.

She was pleased when her father was asked to be on the parish council. That was a good day. A bad day was when he was turned down by the Citizens' Advice Bureau who didn't, according to him, have any idea of the benefits to be conferred by the valuable contributions of a leader of men.

I was more than glad that Jenny came often to swim in our pool. Much as I loved it and our garden myself, I sometimes felt a little sad, when I lay on the grass sunbathing after a swim, that all this had come my way at a time of life when I no longer wished to flaunt the results. I thanked God for the deep peace of the double bed, and took vicarious pleasure in anything I could do to cheer Jenny, still at an age to be as smooth as a sea-washed pebble on a beach. I always swam in a leotard, having had the good sense to throw out my last bikini with my last box of Tampax.

Now that I would never see sixty again, and Charlie a few years older, which worried me as I knew I couldn't

14

bear life without him, it was a comfort to find some advantages in old age.

One was that I didn't mind, as I once did, what opinion people had of me. I preferred to be liked rather than disliked, but I was no longer jealous of anyone else's appearance. If I had had a friend like Jenny when I was young, I would have minded her shapely bosom, her dark blue eyes with their spectacular lashes, and compared them with my own figure and features to my disadvantage. As it was, I could simply enjoy looking at so pretty a creature, and feel the better for having her as my friend.

It saddened me that her first sexual experience had been so calamitous and so loveless. I naturally never told her about my own. I was, to her, so much the long-time and beloved wife of Charlie that she looked up to me in that capacity, and it was no time to tell her anything of what had gone before. Anyway, I was perfectly certain (I am sure rightly so) that reminiscent revelations by over-sixties are embarrassing to the very young. So, no more about it, except that it was a passionate ecstasy, albeit ending in total disaster.

Although she couldn't get away from Littlefold, the one thing Jenny *could* do was to change her job. It was less hassle to accept her father's annoyance at her desertion of his friend the estate agent than to explain to him why she was doing it, and risk his marching in to demand the instant dismissal of her dud ex-lover.

The only job she could get, her expectations not being high, was waitressing in a restaurant which, although it was in the same town as the estate agent's, had the advantage of being at the far end of the High Street.

Bill Patterson was very annoyed, claiming that he hadn't paid for an expensive education to have his daughter end up as a waitress.

Jenny was actually a lot happier in her waitressing job

than she had ever been before. Many of the customers were what she called 'old' and she enjoyed making their dishes look appetising and not overloaded. The less they ate, and the older they were, the more generously they tipped. In a while, she had in her bedroom a jar full of pound coins.

Quite soon I had a surprising encounter with Margaret Patterson. It was difficult really to tell what was wrong with her. Clearly it sounded as though she was very depressed. Having gone through the menopause myself without a blink (it was a long time before that I had learnt that I would definitely have no babies, so that was already behind us and forgotten) I wondered if, being past child-bearing age, that was the cause of Margaret's unhappiness. Maybe she regretted having no son.

Jenny had a touching faith in me. She asked if I would go to see her mother. 'I don't think so,' I said. 'Everyone knows I never drop in on people, so she'd wonder why now?' In the end I suggested that Jenny might like to bring her over one day to sit by the pool with me while Jenny had her swim.

'I'd better bring a swimsuit then,' said Jenny, 'or she'll be shocked. I'll bag Sally's. She can't get into it now, she's too fat since she had the baby.' There was a faint note of satisfaction in her voice. 'She's usually asleep in the afternoon, my mother, I mean. It can't be good for her and I know she doesn't sleep well at night. I often hear her moving about.'

Margaret was very quiet, watching Jenny in the pool. I offered her a cigarette but she said, 'No, thank you. I don't smoke.'

'I know I shouldn't,' I said, really just for something to say, 'but I find it's very nerve-soothing at times.'

'I've sometimes wished I smoked. But of course, we don't. Bill absolutely hates cigarettes.'

Again for something to say, I asked her if she would like to go into the pool herself. 'I could lend you a swim-suit,' I said, 'not very elegant, merely decent.' To my amazement, she jumped at the suggestion.

I took her up to our bedroom to change. 'What a nice room,' she said.

'Terribly untidy, I'm afraid.' Charlie never hangs any-thing up, and I'm not very good at it myself. Our bed-room looks like the opening scene in that play I loved, *A Bequest To The Nation.*

Margaret looked at the shameful muddle with a slightly odd expression on her face. 'We sleep in separate rooms now. I've become so restless at night that poor Bill was being kept awake. So it's better that way.'

I expected to see her going foot by foot down the steps at the shallow end of the pool, and bobbing about keep-ing her un-capped head well out of the water. But no. She walked straight up to the deep end, and went in with the cleanest dive I have ever seen. She shot the length of the pool under water, swimming like a cormorant, kick-turned, and then did at least twenty more lengths, only occasionally raising her head to take in air and go under again. Jenny leant her elbows back over the side of the pool and looked as astonished as I was.

When Margaret at last came out of the pool, Jenny said, 'I didn't know you could swim, Mummy.'

'I taught you, didn't I?' said Margaret.

'Yes. But you just used to walk beside us and hold our chins.'

'I know. It's what mothers do.'

She was rubbing her hair with a towel as she spoke. I said, 'Would you like a glass of wine? I'm going to have one. Orange juice for you, Jenny?' Jenny is always very good about driving. I poured a glass for each of us. Margaret sipped hers slowly, with an air of quiet enjoy-

17

ment. We none of us made any further reference to her virtuoso performance as a swimmer. I was beginning to like this woman, not only for being Jenny's mother, but also for herself. Even so, I had no intention of getting to know her any better.

4

I did invite Margaret to come swimming again, for I was sure it would do her good. But she only came once. I could almost have believed I had imagined the sight of her making the water her own as she had, but for the fact that Jenny had seen it as well.

It was for Jenny's sake that I dragged Charlie along to a drinks party at the Pattersons. Although I had avoided a good many, I had been to enough Littlefold parties to recognise the format.

They always started at 6.30, and ended at 7.45, and were attended largely by the *ancien regime*, who looked at their watches for fear of missing their TV programmes. The entertainment at these gatherings veered between what everyone had seen on the box the night before and what I called the Organ Recital, hips and hearts and hysterectomies. Most of the gatherers were so old that the hysterectomies were those of daughters and daughters-in-law. Such 'young people' as turned up were well and truly married sons and daughters.

On that occasion, the summer weather being excellent, it was an outdoor party. Margaret's mother, Mrs Wallingford, was staying for a few days with her daughter and son-in-law. Jenny had to address her as Grandmother and not Granny. Mrs Wallingford was quite tall, taller than her daughter. Although well into her eighties, her carriage was ramrod straight and upright. Now she was holding a champagne flute in her well-manicured fingers.

19

'This,' she said, glancing accusingly over my shoulder at where Colonel Patterson was standing, 'is not champagne.' She was right. I had seen the bottles myself, obscured in the kitchen. Margaret, who had just introduced me to her mother, was still beside us, holding a glass of orange juice. 'You would do well to avoid this,' said Mrs Wallingford, holding the despised glass aloft, 'it's rather undrinkable.'

I said nothing, and swallowed my drink. It seemed all right to me, but I'm no connoisseur. Bill Patterson was not a great glass-filler, so towards the end of the party I followed Margaret into the kitchen and asked her if I might take a little more of the sparkling whatever-it-was. Margaret poured herself some more of the turgid orange juice, and then I was pleased to see her put it down beside a bottle of vodka, of which she unscrewed the cap, and then added a generous measure to the glass.

Naturally I made no comment. I was simply glad to see the poor woman allowing herself a bit of cheer. For all that the guests would soon be departing, she had a long evening ahead of her with Bill and her mother, who had not struck me as being the easiest of women.

The next day, Jenny came over for a swim. I asked if she had enjoyed the party. 'Er, yes,' she said, 'but poor Mummy's always in a dither when Grandmother comes to stay. She and my father don't get on, which makes Mummy terribly nervous. The only thing they agree on is that I'm a disgrace, being a waitress. They're both terrific snobs.'

I had the feeling that Mrs Wallingford's snobbery had its basis in a grander past than that of Colonel Patterson, which might well have had something to do with their mutual animosity.

A day or two later, I bumped into Margaret and her mother in the village. 'I hear,' said Mrs Wallingford, 'that you have a lovely garden. I would so like to have a garden but, living in a flat as I do, I have to make the best of a balcony.' This left me no alternative but to invite Margaret to bring her over to lunch one day.

As the weather turned cold and windy, we had to make do with a cursory inspection of the garden, after which I was faced with the jaw-aching task of making indoor conversation for two hours.

I am quite certain that Mrs Wallingford had been told that Charlie and I do not have any children. But that didn't stop her from asking, 'Have you grandchildren?' I told her I had not, being myself childless. 'What a pity. Children are the great joy of married life.' Her particular joy had perked up slightly now that I had insisted she have a glass of wine. 'How very sad that must have been for you,' Mrs Wallingford continued. 'These days they do all sorts of things for infertility, don't they?' I would have liked to change the subject, but she was not the one to let go. 'There was probably some simple thing wrong with you that could easily have been put right.'

I had no intention of telling her that the botched abortion I had let myself in for long before I was married to Charlie had made a mess that could never be put right. 'It was no great loss,' I said hardily. 'It allowed me to have a happy marriage *and* a career which I very much enjoyed.'

'*My* career was being the wife of Brigadier Wallingford,' she capped. 'And what was yours?'

'I was in advertising.'

'How very interesting. I would never have been allowed to do such a thing. But then I was fortunate enough to be a debutante in the days when that still meant something. Still, I suppose working in the advertising trade wasn't as bad as what Jenny is doing.'

It had to be temper-keeping time, so I bit back my opinion that Jenny was a very good waitress. I knew, because

I had been to have lunch at the Casuarina Tree. I had an excellent meal and met two of Jenny's fellow waiters, Dick and Desmond, who clearly adored her. So I merely said, 'I thoroughly enjoyed my job, and what's more I was very well paid which is why, between us, Charlie and I could buy this house and live in it in comfort.'

I have to say I was almost sorry when Mrs Wallingford's visit came to an end, she was so gloriously awful. After that cold, windy day the weather improved, so I begged Margaret to come for a swim and bring her mother. This time, Margaret brought with her the swimsuit she must have worn when teaching her girls to swim. She also brought a slightly perished bathing cap.

I led Mrs Wallingford to a seat and waited to enjoy the almost Olympic spectacle of Margaret in the pool. But this time, she clambered in at the shallow end, walked, paddling her hands until the water was up to her waist, then swam a stately breast stroke for a couple of lengths. At last she turned on her back, and I expected to see her arms circling in a back-crawl. But she kept them at her side, just flapping the water and scarcely moving her feet.

'Margaret is such a good swimmer,' I said.

'Oh?' said Mrs Wallingford and went on to tell me how sad the loss of the brigadier had been. He died, it seemed, of cancer of the prostate. 'He was so brave, so stoical. He never complained, he never let on, even to himself, that anything was wrong until it was too late.' She put a clean handkerchief to her eyes and continued, 'If only I'd known, I would have made him go to the doctor much, much sooner. He might still have been alive today.'

'How old would he have been?' I asked sympathetically.

'Well, he was older than me, much older, so he would have been ninety, I suppose. I do beg you to be watchful with your own husband. You must keep an eye on him.'

'I do,' I said truthfully. Mrs Wallingford eventually departed. She was, she told me, longing to get home to her own little nest but she worried about poor Margaret. 'She seems to have no interests. She does almost nothing. At her age, I was indefatigable.'

It was a few days after her mother left that Margaret had an accident which put her into hospital. I got the details from Jenny. Jenny had been doing the lunch and tea shift at the Casuarina Tree, and she had stayed on chatting to her friends Dick and Desmond while they cleared and prepared tables for the evening.

Now that Mrs Wallingford was gone, and her relentless energy with her, Margaret had, it seemed, reverted to her previous habit of spending the afternoon alone in her bedroom.

Jenny found her at the bottom of the stairs. She was alone. 'Daddy was out. He does hospital driving. I asked her how long she had been there, and she said she didn't know, and that she had been looking for something. She had obviously hurt herself, and she was very shocked. So I got the ambulance people, and they were great, so kind. She's got a broken wrist, and her collarbone is out of place and her elbow is chipped.' It seems that the paramedics ushered Jenny into the ambulance with her mother. Jenny does look, in spite of her pretty figure, very young, so that might be why they hadn't seen her as the owner of her own car.

In the end, Jenny found herself transportless at the County Hospital, her mother being, as the nurses put it, rested before impending surgery.

Having eventually said goodnight, Jenny telephoned her father to ask him to come and take her home. He was in quite a state, having come home to find the place like, as he put it, the Marie Céleste.

I went to see Margaret in hospital. She was so gentle

and mannerly that I could easily understand why she was a favourite with the nurses. She had not yet been let out of bed, plastered and strapped as she was from neck to hand. While I was there, the staff nurse came and gave her a pain-killer. She was thanked. 'That nice physiotherapist came this morning,' said Margaret.

'She's keeping your legs moving, so you won't be too wobbly when we get you up,' said the nurse.

I had never seen Margaret so happy, or so relaxed. I went two or three times. Once, I arrived to find Bill Patterson beside her bed. I hovered. 'Still in bed?' I heard him say.

'I have to keep my arm and shoulder still,' said Margaret, 'but the physiotherapist is helping me to exercise my legs.'

An Indian doctor, a woman I had seen before, came over and said a smiling Hallo to Bill Patterson. Then, to Margaret, she said, 'How are you today?'

'I'm still in a lot of pain, I'm afraid.' It struck me as slightly odd that Margaret, usually so uncomplaining, should say this.

'It was a nasty break,' said the doctor sympathetically.

'Not surprising,' said Bill, who fortunately seemed to realise that the woman *was* a doctor and not a nurse. He continued, with apparent jocularity, 'I don't seem to be able to turn my back for five minutes without you falling downstairs.'

'It was silly of me,' said Margaret.

'How did it happen?' asked the doctor.

Bill elected to be the answerer. 'I'm afraid I don't know. I was out at the time, as I've said. I do a great deal in the parish, you see. My wife is more – reclusive. Really, dear, you do spend too much time alone in your room.'

'I read a lot,' said Margaret.

The doctor, looking slightly nonplussed, nevertheless moved on to her next patient. Soon after, Bill left the ward. Before going, he leaned over Margaret as though to kiss her. She turned her face aside. Bill looked hurt and walked away, stooping slightly.

Margaret went to sleep. For all that I didn't much like Bill Patterson, I did feel a little sorry for him on this occasion.

5

Even though Bill explained to the doctor that it was very difficult for him to look after his wife adequately, she was sent home while still bandaged up. When I went to see her at home, I wished she had been kept in hospital longer. The plaster of Paris was fretting her in the hot weather and she was miserable with feeling helpless and useless.

She scarcely stirred outside the house. Only with difficulty could I get her to join me in a stroll round the garden.

Clearly Bill Patterson's interest in domesticity did not extend to the chores which someone had to do now that Margaret was utterly useless, so Jenny was obliged to take time off from work to look after her mother, and to run the house.

There were the usual offers from neighbours of, 'If there is anything I can do, please let me know.' But since everyone was well aware that Jenny was there (after all, giving up that sort of job to look after her mother wasn't much of a sacrifice) no one felt it necessary to take any actual action. Visitors were few.

'Dick and Desmond have been over twice,' said Jenny. 'It's so kind of them.' I suspected that Dick and Desmond came more on account of Jenny than of her mother.

On one occasion their car pulled up just as I was getting out of mine. 'Hallo, Mrs Finlay,' they cried. I would have been quite happy to have them call me Annie, but they rather enjoyed their *maître d'* act. 'Lovely to see you. We're prison visiting too,' said Desmond.

'What *do* you mean?' I asked.

'Darling Jenny, of course,' said Dick. 'That old monster of a father. Just when Jenny's so happy in her work.'

'I don't think he means any harm,' I said. 'He just feels a bit helpless. Men don't know how to nurse, after all.' As a matter of fact, Charlie had spent a fortnight only the previous winter nursing me through a bad bout of 'flu, even including the gastric period of it.

We went in and up to Margaret's bedroom, accompanied by Jenny. Dick and Desmond produced a bottle of champagne, and removed the wire while Jenny went to get glasses, which they rapidly filled.

By the time we all left, the level in the glasses had scarcely lowered. Jenny came downstairs with us, saw us out of the front door and went inside again. At the gate, Dick said, 'She'll finish that lot up, now we're gone.'

For the second time that day, I said 'What *do* you mean?'

'She's secret. We know these things. We've seen it all,' said Desmond.

'But she doesn't drink very much. I've only once made her have a glass of wine at my house,' I said, pushing away the memory of Margaret's furtive addition of vodka to her orange juice at the party. I didn't want to hear any more, so I mumbled something about missing car keys and turned back.

I rang the door bell. 'Sorry, Jenny,' I said, 'but I think I must have left my car keys in your mother's room.' I went upstairs, knocked and entered. The glasses were still full. Maybe she was very cunning? 'Oh, Margaret,' I said, 'how silly, I thought I'd left my car keys, but they're here in my pocket all the time. You haven't touched your champagne. Do try, it will do you good.' I lifted a glass myself, and put one in Margaret's hand. She swallowed it down. 'I'll put the rest back in the bottle,' she said. 'Jenny can get me one of those plastic stoppers Bill keeps in the drinks cupboard later.' I left.

August was giving way to September. 'This bloody grass,' said Charlie. 'It never stops growing.' I dead-headed a few roses and persuaded him to abandon the lawn-mower and sit down. 'Are you going to have a swim?' he asked. 'I'm so sweaty I might join you.'

'Do you think Margaret Patterson is a secret drinker?' I asked.

Charlie burst out laughing. 'I wouldn't blame her if she was. I would be, if I had to live with pompous Patterson.'

'Dick and Desmond seem to think so,' I said.

'The Gay Hussars,' said Charlie. 'I love them.' He had met them on occasions when he had taken me to dinner at the Casuarina Tree.

'Tempted?' I asked.

'Not really. It's a long time since I left school. But I do like them. They're efficient and they are quite remarkably observant. If I'd still been in the ad business, I bet I could have found a use for them.'

I never did find out what happened to the rest of the champagne.

I tried not to worry about Jenny. I hoped she would get back soon to the job that gave her so much satisfaction, but I was gloomily aware that her father would pull against it for as long as he could.

6

I've always quite enjoyed the safe boringness of Littlefold, even to the extent of getting involved, sometimes. My dahlias won third prize in the flower show. My dahlias were small and pointy and were beaten by things that looked like red cabbages. I behaved well and admired the winning entries in the manner adopted by Oscar runners-up.

All this was fine but I did sometimes long for a breath of fresh air. Charlie was perfectly content, thank God, being one of those rare people who is able to determine what he wants, go out and get it, and be happy with it. He has also always had an additional, enviable talent, that of saying no. He was very much liked in Littlefold, as everything he did was done with the good grace which is only possible if you know how to reject what you don't want to do.

I tried to emulate him, but being a female was against me, and was why it was sometimes almost impossible to avoid being caught up in matters that I found tedious. So I was very pleased to receive a telephone call from my erstwhile employee, Peter Baker. I had seen him from time to time after I gave up my job to move to Littlefold with Charlie. He had been down to visit us a few times, and I had had more than one riotous lunch with him in London.

'Hallo, Peter,' I said happily. 'How are you and what are you doing?'

'I'm sitting on my balcony having a spritzer,' he said. Peter has a highly desirable riverside apartment. It's a long time since he first came to me as a seventeen-year-old apprentice, as ignorant of syntax as any puppy of house-training. His form of illiteracy was a welcome relief after some of the graduates in English I had interviewed when seeking promising beginners. Even thirty years ago, they made me feel old with their complacent contempt for the grammar they had avoided learning.

So, when Peter came my way, with clear and unmistakable signs of advertising talent, I took him on. After a few years with me, we both agreed that he should move on, which he had done with great success.

Peter was now a Creative Director. Although, at my advanced age, I was sure I had left all thoughts of the advertising business behind me, I felt a sudden pang of envy, and admitted it.

So I was a little surprised to hear him say, 'I'm supposed to be going out to dinner tonight but I am going to duck it. It's advertising people, and I'm bored stiff with them. I'm bored stiff, Annie. Bored and old.'

'Have a heart,' I said, 'don't talk old to me, you're barely forty.'

'I've been around too long. The last judging panel I was on, I couldn't understand a single word of the commercials we were looking at.'

'Something wrong with your sex life?' I asked rudely.

'Oh no. That's all right.' Although Peter never re-married after his early and short-lived connubial effort with poor pretty Italian Maria, he has never suffered from an empty bed. He was hotly contested for, married ladies a speciality. 'I get plenty of that. It's just advertising. Oh, for the days of PILES ARE PAINFUL.'

We both laughed in recollection of the very first advertisement I had made him write. I said, 'And you thought your first assignment was going to be naked houris eating coconut chocolate on a tropical island.'

'Naked houris? Naked haemorrhoids, more like. I couldn't even spell it. Hang on a tick while I fill my glass. Oh, to hell with the soda water.' I heard the pleasant sound of wine glugging into what sounded like a tumbler. 'Since I'm damn well not going out I may as well get drunk. I'll tell you one thing, Annie, I'm dead popular with my department. If ever we get a nice old-fashioned client who wants a comprehensible eight-inch double, I do it myself. Those little buggers couldn't write their way out of a paper bag. How's Charlie?'

'He's well, thank you. They've let him become a bell-ringer, but he's very junior, he's only learning. He calls himself tail-end Charlie. I hope he doesn't crock his back again.'

'May I come and see you, Annie? I need you.'

There is no surer way to a woman's heart than being needed by a handsome young male friend. Well, forty is young to me. 'Come at once,' I said. 'The weather's lovely and the pool is warm.'

'Not this minute. I'm getting drunk. May I come on Saturday morning, please?'

'Do you want to bring anyone with you?' I asked. Our guest room was double-bed. I didn't really want one of Peter's sophisticated females, but I feared he might be bored with just us.

Charlie had a Rover and I had a dear little Deux-Chevaux. Charlie called it my invalid car but it suited me for the short distances I covered. The car in which Peter pulled up was very grand indeed by comparison.

'I didn't bring you flowers,' said Peter, hugging me. 'There was no point, when you've got all this. And I know Charlie keeps a good cellar, so I didn't insult him. I brought you this instead.'

'This' was a good-sized jar of caviar. Veritable Beluga. I had bought guineafowl. I always buy guineafowl when we have someone to dinner, largely because it is Charlie's favourite, and it is a good excuse to cook it for him, with apple and raisin stuffing.

Caviar put a different complexion on the day. I suddenly thought of Jenny. If anyone deserved a little diversion, and some conversation beyond a sick mother and an oppressive father, it was she. And I was morally certain she had never tasted caviar. 'Caviar,' I said, 'Oh, Peter, what a treat. Lucky I've got a lemon.'

I went to the telephone. To my surprise, it was answered by Margaret. I said, 'Oh, Margaret.' One always says 'Oh' when nonplussed. 'I wonder if Jenny would like to come over for a swim this evening and stay on for supper. Could you manage without her?'

'Of course I could.'

'Will you be all right for supper?'

'Of course,' Margaret repeated, and added, 'Jenny always gives me lunch and I really need very little after that.'

'Will Bill be all right?' I didn't care about Bill, but I asked for Margaret's sake.

'He can get something for himself if he wants it,' said Margaret with unwonted sturdiness. 'What time would you like Jenny to come?'

'About six o'clock. Then she can have a swim first of all. We've got an old friend visiting, so it would be very nice if she could come.'

Knowing we had company, Jenny turned up in a freshly ironed and pretty though rather old-fashioned frock. She had also brought her sister Sally's swimsuit.

I was concerned about basting the guineafowl and finding a smart enough bowl to fill with cracked ice for the caviar. So I suggested to Peter (I wanted both him and

Charlie out of the way while I was in the kitchen) that he join Jenny in the pool. Charlie was, as usual, not in the swimming mood, so I left him watching sport on television.

Once everything in the kitchen was doing as well as I could hope for, I collected Charlie and went side by side with him down to the pool.

Sally's swimsuit was a good deal too large for Jenny. As she swam, it almost came off. Charlie whispered 'Phew' in my ear.

Peter very neatly pulled the straps up over Jenny's shoulders.

Jenny was rather quiet during dinner but not because she was bored. She only spoke to ask Peter questions about advertising, hanging on his every word.

I restrained my slightly jealous desire to explain that I was the person who had taught Peter his trade. But I need not have concerned myself. 'Ask Annie about the business,' said Peter, 'if you're thinking of it for yourself. All I can tell you is that she taught me. And she and Charlie were the famous advertising couple. Married through thick and thin. Quite remarkable.'

'Is your wife in advertising, too?' asked Jenny.

'I haven't got a wife, not now,' said Peter.

7

Littlefold was, and probably always will be, an us-and-them village. Although I had grown up in a place very much like it, it took me quite a while to readjust, after so many years of an entirely different way of life, to its mores. Those who considered themselves to be Littlefold gentry, especially those over a certain age had, of course, an impeccable past, and villainy, if they were to be believed, was confined to the council houses. The gentry themselves believed in the Church, Her Majesty The Queen, and marriage.

It was also the general idea that real Littlefold families had been there forever. Bill Patterson, although I don't believe he bought his house much before we bought ours, certainly acted in this manner.

Charlie, being Charlie, and the most unself-conscious, as well as the nicest, man I have ever known, fitted easily in from the word go. I survived by keeping a low profile and relishing my respectable life.

I only really got into cooking in our Littlefold years. I wanted to do it earlier, when I was in my first real love, but that was not to be. And, during my London years with Charlie, we ate out a lot, and took people out or had caterers, so I had hardly any experience of housekeeping, and was hopeless at it. On balance, the thing I missed most when I left my working years behind me was leaving the house in one state and returning to find it in another, and much better one. Charlie said he admired the chutz-

34

pah of a woman who could learn cooking and gardening from scratch, but not housework.

Peter was staying over until Sunday evening. I had arranged to have an early lunch, so that he could enjoy a glass of wine and then have a long pause before a cup of tea preceding the drive back to London.

I was slightly surprised, while we were drinking our morning coffee in the garden, to see Jenny arriving. But she had, after all, been told that she was welcome to come for a swim whenever she wanted to. She gave me a kiss and said, 'Annie, thank you so much for last night. It was a lovely evening. And your food!' Although she had enjoyed the caviar, she had not eaten greedily, and had not in fact had much at all after that, having obviously been absorbed in the conversation. Even so, she now said, 'May I have a swim? I need to work off all that pigginess.'

I nodded yes of course, and she slipped off the cotton shirt and shorts that covered Sally's swimsuit. 'Are you coming in, Peter?' she asked. Peter went indoors to get changed, and I decided that I would join them in the pool. Lunch was cold, and already prepared. I swam briskly up and down, which meant that Jenny and Peter had to take their places either side of me. The swimsuit did slip a little, but Jenny carefully straightened it up again.

After the swim, we sat in the sun until we had all got dry. Jenny was not at all flirtatious with Peter. Looking at him, I noticed that he was not as lean as he once had been. He had come my way all those years ago as a skinny boy. His origins had not endowed him with any breadth of shoulder, and he had not had the sort of schooling that builds strong thighs and chest muscles. So, although still far from being fat, there was an inch of fleshiness above his bathing trunks which, had he been a woman, would have precluded the wearing of a tucked-in silk shirt.

He was kind, almost paternal, with Jenny. 'Do you have a job?' he asked.

'I do. But I've had to give it up for the time being,' she said. 'My mother isn't very well. She had an accident and broke some bones.'

'What is your job when you're at it?'

'Nothing much, though I like it, and I like the people I work with. I work in a restaurant. They do let me in the kitchen a bit, but really I'm only a waitress.'

I interjected. 'It's a very good restaurant, and Jenny is much thought of there. The customers love her, and so do the staff.'

'What is the restaurant called?' asked Peter. Jenny told him it was called the Casuarina Tree and he said, 'That's a good name; catchy. I often think that naming an interesting product is the only fun left in advertising.'

Charlie came out and joined us with a tray of glasses and a jug of my home-made lemonade. The ice made a pleasant sound as he poured. Peter who, although he was only forty, was going rather grey in the hair, accepted his drink and began to walk about. I recognised this old habit of his. He had always walked about when a subject interested him. 'In my opinion,' he said, 'a good restaurant is a terrific project.'

'That or an Old Folks' Home,' said I.

'Oh really, Annie. Now, Jenny. If you are apprenticing yourself to the restaurant business, the world's your oyster. I've half a mind to go in for it myself, one of these days. You could be my chef.'

Jenny blushed and said, 'Don't be silly. I'm far off being a chef.' But she looked pleased, just the same.

'I was pretty far off being an adman when I apprenticed myself to Annie,' he replied.

'Have you seen Annie's Albertine?' asked Jenny. My

36

Albertine is a great rose, blooming as it does two or more times in the year, and Jenny led the way to show it to Peter, chatting and listening as they went, Jenny doing most of the listening, for it was obvious that she was riveted to every word spoken by Peter.

I was contemplating inviting her to stay for lunch when the telephone rang. I rushed into the house to answer it. 'Bill Patterson,' it said. 'Is Jenny with you?'

'Yes. She's just been having a swim.'

'Oh, good. Thank you for allowing her. Perhaps she has forgotten that her sister and her sister's husband and their little boy are arriving for lunch in half an hour. And her mother is not able to cook a meal.'

I refrained from suggesting that Sally might do something about it, and went to fetch Jenny. '*Had* you forgotten that Sally was coming today?' I asked. She looked vague.

Then, 'I'd better go, hadn't I? There's a steak and kidney pie in the freezer.'

'There speaks the inspired restaurateur,' said Peter.

'I'm certainly not driving anywhere today,' said Charlie during lunch, quietly pouring the wine. I joined him. Peter, remaining with the lemonade and some mineral water, decided to leave a little earlier than I had expected. 'I daren't stay,' he said, 'I enjoy myself too much.'

'Don't you want some tea?' I asked.

'No, thank you. I'd best get back. For as long as I'm staying in the business, I'd better prepare for tomorrow.'

'Did you like my friend Jenny?' I asked.

'She's enchanting.'

Shortly after Peter left, it clouded over. We had said goodbye to him and begged him to come again. The day darkened, and it began to rain quite heavily. 'Good for the garden,' I said.

Charlie said, 'I'm worn out with visitors.'

'You!' I said scornfully. 'What do you do about it?'

'Just have them,' he said. 'It's going to get cold, too. Come to bed.' So I did, though it was a long way off nightfall.

I was wakened by the sound of banging doors and windows, so I got up and went round the house closing them. 'Could we have some scrambled eggs?' said Charlie when I returned. I made them and we ate them in the kitchen.

Although I've been doing my own entertaining for years now, I still always seem to need reassurance. 'Was dinner last night all right?' I asked.

'Yes indeed. The guineafowl was first-rate. One of your best stuffings, too. Peter enjoyed it. He really is a very nice chap.'

'He was very sweet with Jenny,' I said. 'I'm glad for her to meet someone interesting for a change.'

'She's interested all right, I can tell you.'

'Oh, not like that,' I said, 'he's years older than her. More like an uncle.'

'You didn't hear what I heard,' said Charlie. It seemed that Jenny had asked Peter if he was coming down again, and when he said no, not in the foreseeable future, she had gone on to announce that she sometimes went to London to see friends (it was the first I'd heard of it) and could she come and see him when she was up? 'I know she's not our responsibility,' Charlie continued, 'but she does have very old-fashioned parents, and we do know them, and she *is* a very attractive girl. So think. If she lands in Peter's lap, I'd hardly blame him for taking the opportunity.'

'I find it hard to believe,' I said. 'He's so much older than her. But then, I suppose it might not be a bad thing.' Then I told Charlie the story of Jenny's dismal experience earlier.

'Oh well,' he said, 'it wouldn't do much damage then,

and she might get some enjoyment. Harmless enough, as long as she doesn't look on Peter as a lasting proposition.'

8

Not having children of my own, I have long consoled myself by imagining their grown-up disapproval of their mother. Peter was not my only old friend from advertising days. I was also in touch with quite a few of my female ex-colleagues. They, to a woman, all seemed to have children who regarded smoking as a capital offence, and the eating of anything that didn't taste of unsalted straw (To-fu or whatever that frightful stuff is called) as tantamount to throwing yourself under a lorry. One of my old friends even had an American daughter-in-law who wouldn't eat a biscuit unless she had first read the packet for criminal content. But Jenny, who was my friend, had always given me her affection and an admiration which, although it was probably undeserved, did my self-esteem a lot of good.

I was, however, becoming concerned for her, particularly as I was aware that she had not been able to return to her job at the Casuarina Tree. I called on Margaret from time to time. September had given way to October. The Michaelmas daisies in our garden were particularly good that year. I asked Margaret if she had Michaelmas daisies in her garden, but she didn't know whether she had or not. Her plaster-casts were long dispensed with but she didn't seem to be gaining any energy. While September was still with us, Jenny had continued swimming, but Margaret had not joined her.

There was a helplessly guilty air about her. 'I don't

know what I would do without Jenny,' she said, 'I'd be lost without her. But I'm afraid it's a very dull existence for a young girl.'

'Perhaps,' I said, 'you might suggest that she goes back to work at the Casuarina Tree.' Jenny never spoke of Peter, but her face would light up whenever I mentioned his name. And there was far too little to distract her from thinking about him.

'I suppose we should,' said Margaret, 'but you know Bill has never liked her working there. He was very annoyed when she left her proper job. It really upsets him to have his daughter a waitress, and he doesn't like her friends Dick and Desmond.'

I liked Dick and Desmond a good deal. I still went to the Casuarina Tree, sometimes for lunch, sometimes for dinner, and both Charlie and I found Dick and Desmond's cheery company preferable to that of Bill Patterson.

'I really ought not to cling to her so,' said Margaret. 'Maybe she could get her secretarial job back again.' I could hardly think of that as a very good idea, and even Margaret added, 'but I don't think she was very happy there.' So she had observed that much. Otherwise, there was a sort of emotional distance about her, as though she was wrapped in clingfilm.

I was sorry for Margaret up to a point, but I couldn't help feeling slightly irritated by her retreat. There was Jenny, stuck at home to run a house in which her mother spent as much time as she could in her own room. On the occasions when I went up there to see her, I was aware that she kept a radio babbling away. 'Are you enjoying this play?' I asked, and added that I very much liked the actor who was playing the lead. But clearly she hadn't been listening to any of it.

I debated the hints I had been given that Margaret was prone to secret tippling. But I couldn't see how this could

41

be. She hardly ever left the house, so I could see no way in which she could possibly be assembling a hoard of booze under her bed. The evidence was that she simply kept to her room because she was miserable.

Jenny was stuck, day in and day out, in this utterly depressing household. I was becoming so incensed that I decided Bill Patterson ought to be tackled. I told Charlie that I was going to see him, and tell him face to face how very unfair this all was on Jenny, and that the least he could do was to get a housekeeper, if he wasn't prepared to do a bit more himself, and let Jenny get back to work.

'That,' said Charlie, 'is probably one of the worst ideas you've had since the day you suggested to Domestos that they call a toilet-cleanser a shit-shifter.'

'Well,' I said in my defence, 'it was after a big lunch.'

'Yes. But seriously, darling, you'll do more harm than good if you interfere. Apart from anything else, can't you see how Bill would look at it? In his view you'd be telling him to hire a domestic in order to let Jenny go out to work in what he would see as exactly that capacity.'

I had to take his point. Meanwhile, a diversion presented itself. Charlie had a sister who had gone to Australia years ago, married a farmer, and had been out there ever since. We were expecting a visit from her grandson, whose name we knew to be Gareth. It was to be Gareth's first visit to Europe and he needed a base in what Charlie's sister now referred to as the UK. So we had naturally said he must stay with us.

We met him at Heathrow. He was a good-looking, likeable young man with pleasant manners. We were having the usual November weather, which he took in his stride. 'Gran told me it would be foggy all the time, so it doesn't surprise me,' he said. Actually, there wasn't what I would call a fog, but then, Charlie's sister had left England in the days when we still had smog.

I certainly wasn't trying to match-make. My main hope was that somehow or other Jenny could be got back to work. But I did hope this pleasant young man would at least take her mind off Peter, from whom nothing had been heard since his visit to us. It was a forlorn hope.

In Littlefold, the arrival of a young visitor, especially a young, single, masculine visitor, was as welcome as the arrival of mail, medicine and fresh meat would have been to explorers lost up the Amazon. Gareth was clearly quite taken with Jenny, and she certainly didn't dislike him.

So it was a natural thing that she and Gareth should get to know each other. Jenny went so far as to abandon her home duties now and then to drive Gareth round our countryside, beautiful even in this winter weather. He didn't mind the weather, it was right for England in his view, but he was rather puzzled to find that Buckingham Palace and Land's End couldn't be included in a day trip.

I asked him what he thought of Jenny's parents. 'Nice folks,' he said, 'the Colonel's a great old guy, isn't he? I know lots like him at home.'

'Do you?' I asked. I had not visualised Bill Patterson in connection with breezy, republican Australia.

'Oh sure. At the RSL. My grandfather's in the RSL.' On asking for an explanation of these initials, I learnt that they stood for Returned Servicemen's League, the equivalent of our British Legion.

Margaret seemed to come as no surprise to him. I really knew little about Australian women, beyond those adventurous ex-pats I had met in advertising; a bossy, critical bunch. But I could only suppose that there were many Margarets in Gareth's milieu. Gareth was so intrigued by Jenny that he contemplated staying on with us (forever, it seemed) rather than pursuing his discovery of Ireland, France, and the rest of Europe.

43

Under the influence of Littlefold and what he saw as respectable old Auntie Annie and Uncle Charlie, Gareth treated Jenny with positively Victorian respect. This was a pity. I asked him if he had a girlfriend at home. 'Oh, lots of them, Australia is different from here,' he said, with the sweeping assurance of the new arrival in the old country.

My dear Charlie has always considered that a visit of one night is quite enough, two pushing it. 'Guests,' he quoted on this occasion, unoriginally, 'are like fish. They stink after the third day.'

I don't suppose we would ever have parted with Gareth had it not been for the surprise.

I don't quite know why Peter walked into it as he did. Jenny was pretty, dear and charming, but Peter did not need any complications in his already lady-filled life.

It was early in December. As Jenny came into the house with Gareth, the telephone was ringing. I can't remember where they had been that day. Gareth was helping her off with her coat, still ridiculously courtly. I answered the telephone.

'Annie,' said Peter, 'do you have the Pattersons' telephone number?'

'Yes,' I said, reluctantly, but as Jenny was near enough to hear every word, I was obliged to add, 'if you want Jenny, she's here at the moment. Would you like to speak to her?'

Jenny remained standing during the conversation. I could see her legs shaking as she spoke. 'Oh. Yes. I'd love to. When?' Whatever date was being made, there was no need for me to hand her pencil and paper. Obviously, any arrangement was about to be engraved unerasably on Jenny's mind. 'No, I won't drive up. I've never driven in London, and I know I'd get lost. I'll get the train. No, no, no. No need to meet me. I'll take a taxi. Well, thank you,

44

I'd love to. Would you like me to come a bit early so I can help?'

Eventually she rang off and turned to me with an expression on her face that Gareth would have given his best surf-board and his skis for. 'That was Peter,' she said, as though I didn't know. 'He's giving a party and he wants me to come. It'll go on very late, so he says I'm to stay over. He has a spare room. There'll be all sorts of people there. And he thought I might enjoy it. He thought of me, Annie.'

I then found that this party was taking place quite soon. Gareth would still be with us, and he had not yet been to London. I felt mean, knowing what I was about to say, but I believed I should at least try to act the part of a grown-up. 'Perhaps,' I said, 'you might ask Peter if you could bring Gareth. It wouldn't make a difference, as it's a big party. And you and Gareth could spend the day in London before it. And,' I gabbled this bit, 'you wouldn't need to stay the night. I can quite see Peter thought you shouldn't come home by train, so late, by yourself. But with Gareth...'

'No!' Jenny snapped the word. More politely, she added, 'He didn't say anything about bringing anybody else. I couldn't, Annie, I couldn't. Gareth can do something by himself. He can have my car if he likes.'

Gareth heard this clearly. Not long after, he decided to cut his stay with us short. When he left, he merely said 'Ciao,' and that was the last we heard of him.

'I suppose,' said Charlie, 'it isn't only Australians who don't write bread and butter letters these days.'

9

'So did she sleep with him?' asked Charlie.

'I haven't the faintest idea,' I replied, austerely. Jenny had returned from London looking extremely happy. She was just in time to say goodbye to Gareth, which she did with kindly equanimity. 'I'll give you a bell some time,' said Gareth.

'Please do,' said Jenny, good manners for 'Don't bother'.

Charlie, I happened to know, was preparing a surprise present for me for Christmas. This involved my having to pretend that I had no idea what was going on at the end of the garden. I had never had one of those roll-on covers for the pool, I had always dreaded finding the trapped, drowned corpses of foolish mice under it. And now Charlie was having a pool-house made. I had been very happy to have a pool at all. I wasn't quite certain about this grandeur. But, on the other hand, I could see the enormous advantage of being able to swim year-round. I sometimes felt a little breathless, although unfairly well for a wicked old smoker. I loved Charlie for the thought, although I was a little anxious about feeling shut in. However, I chose a moment when Charlie was out to ask a few questions, from which I learnt that the walls were constructed so that they could be rolled up into themselves in summer time. And the roof was to be of reinforced glass. All I had to do now was to continue to pretend I knew nothing about it, and that workmen trampling down the garden, with timber, tools and frames

46

were invisible. I bit my tongue when I almost asked Charlie if he wanted me to make coffee for the men.

So Christmas was approaching. Littlefold was always in a great tiz about Christmas. Were the young coming? Would a sixteen pound turkey do? All that sort of fuss. I had had varied Christmases in my life. One, long ago, was so lonely that the only post I got was the electricity bill.

Charlie and I had had many a busy Christmas in our advertising days. Since coming to Littlefold, we always talked about going away for Christmas but we never did. I claimed that locking up a country house and ensuring it against freezing up was too complicated. By the other side of the token, we also always talked about going away somewhere in the summer, but by then I claimed it was the nicest time of the year to be at home and I couldn't let the garden go wild. Whatever had happened to the Annie Finlay who once thought nothing of flying out to New York for a meeting and then on down to Barbados to shoot a sunny commercial? I went several times to Hong Kong, on my firm's business, once to Kuala Lumpur, and twice to Tokyo.

Had I become agoraphobic? Maybe. But the difference was that in those days, our working journeys never coincided. If Charlie was away, I was at home, and vice versa. It was a very different thing to return from a jointly taken trip to a house that had been empty while one was away, and reproached one for it for days on end. Being a childless couple, we had the colossal advantage of being able to afford to do and to own things that we wouldn't otherwise have been able to. Plus a quiet life at home; often very quiet.

I told Jenny that something was going on at the bottom of the garden. 'I know,' she said. 'Charlie has told me all about it. But it's a great secret and you are *not to know*.'

47

She was a very happy Jenny at that time. Always pretty, she was now quite beautiful.

I invited her to come and have lunch with me at the Casuarina Tree, but she said, 'No. Thanks, Annie, but I don't want to. Dick and Desmond will only want to know when I'm going back to work there, and I'm not.'

'But surely you could, by now? Your mother could manage, I'm sure.'

'It's not that. I just have other things to think about.' I was fearful. 'It doesn't matter,' she went on. 'I can stay around at home quite happily now. I shall go away for good, one day.'

Through the window, I could see snow beginning to fall. I hoped a snowstorm wouldn't put a stop to work on Charlie's secret. But it was all right. It was typical December snow, tantalising with the prospect of a white Christmas and turning, as usual, into the inevitable tepid slush. 'Has Gareth asked you to go back-packing in India?' I asked, idiotically.

'Gareth?' She might just as well have said, 'Who he?'

Well, I knew the score, of course I did. 'You enjoyed the party, I take it?' I said.

'It was wonderful. I got there quite early, Annie. Peter had bought lots of food. There was caviar, just like he brought down to you. And I made the toast and cut up the lemon.'

'I'm sure there were lots of interesting people there,' I said. But I was not destined to hear much about the interesting people.

'I made omelettes later,' said Jenny. 'I'm glad I can cook.' I didn't think Peter wanted a cook. He had once been married to one, his Italian Maria.

Well as I now knew Jenny, I could scarcely ask so indelicate a question as 'Did you go to bed with him?' But it seemed pretty clear that that had not happened. I know

48

Peter, and he would have regarded my young friend as a 'don't touch'. But the result of his good behaviour was that Jenny now longed for him more than ever, irrevocably in love to a serious extent. I had hoped that her initial crush on Peter was simply the result of a boring and limited existence in Littlefold. And he *had* arrived on her scene trailing the glory of the great world.

I should have known that Jenny was a very different young woman from many of her contemporaries. She was a skin short of the hard streak.

I never heard the words 'having sex' pass her lips, I am happy to say. For her, making love must be just that, love being the operative word. Her first experience had served only to clarify this aspect of Jenny. And love was obviously what she was looking forward to with Peter. Although I had hoped that Gareth might have provided a romantic interest – he was, after all, the right age for her – it was eminently clear that her attention to him had been merely good manners and kindness to our young relation. And I had to admit that now he had gone on his way, he was as forgettable to me as he obviously was to her.

Everything I had learned of Jenny proved her vulnerability. She was quite without the opportunism of her sister Sally, who had married to her own advantage. It was Jenny's lot to fall in love with a forty-year-old divorced man whose main preoccupation in life was his disenchantment with what looked to everyone else like a highly successful career. Peter was not looking for complications.

Charlie's often-mentioned plan for Christmas was that we should tell everyone we were going away and then not go. His ideal was to spend the day in bed with a cold guineafowl, a plate of smoked salmon sandwiches and a bottle or two of wine.

I was surprised when, this year, he proposed that we invite a house-guest. For Charlie to suggest having anyone to stay was unusual to remarkable. If Gareth had not been his sister's grandson, he would have been given leave to depart a good deal sooner, and in plain terms.

So, when Charlie said, 'I've been thinking about Christmas. How about asking Peter down to stay?' my obvious conclusion was that this had to do with celebrating my surprise present. And I knew that Charlie enjoyed Peter's company. They had a lot in common, not least their shared weariness of the advertising trade.

I have to say I thought it a good idea. At least, with Peter as our guest, I could watch over Jenny. I don't know quite how my mind was working. I feared to see her hurt, as I knew she might well, in the long run, be. But I also believed it might be no bad thing to let events take their course, with any luck running it out. There could be no future in her love for Peter. But there, I knew from experience how little future there usually is in early love. I decided to invite Peter, and leave the outcome to chance.

'I'll tell you why,' I said, when I rang Peter to invite him, 'you might think it odd for Charlie to be wanting people to stay, knowing him.'

'I do,' said Peter, 'I felt more than honoured to be let in the house last time.'

'Well,' said I, 'there's a secret, you see,' and I told him about the pool house. Jenny was not mentioned by either of us, at this point, but a few days before Peter was due to arrive, she received a Christmas card that rendered her totally ecstatic. It was the standard, rather art-directorish advertising agency card. The signature was merely 'Peter'. But the intoxicating words, 'May see you at Christmas, I'm coming down to stay with Annie and Charlie for a day or so,' were appended to it.

Peter's visit would certainly enliven our Christmas, and what harm could there be in his enlivening Jenny's as well? Jenny's Christmas Day was destined to consist of cooking, mother-care, baby-care and father-pacifying. Sally, her husband and little boy were coming. I had not long since seen Sally, who was pregnant again, and making a meal of it, crotchety and all set for a feet-up break over the holiday. I took the option of thinking 'Why bother about anything other than that Jenny is going to have a bit of fun for once?' and decided there could be no significance in inviting the whole Patterson family over for cold lunch on Boxing Day.

On Christmas morning, we went to early service, accompanied by a rather surprised Peter. He watched in some awe as Charlie and I took Communion. Afterwards he said, 'The last time I was in a church was when I married Maria, and that didn't do much good, did it?'

Charlie and I had both been confirmed at school. This amazed Peter, who told us over breakfast, 'I never heard of schools doing that. They certainly didn't at Balham Secondary.'

The turkey was cooking slowly. As we were having guests the next day, it was a big one, and as there were only the three of us today, it didn't matter when we should eat. 'Well,' said Peter. 'Well,' said Charlie. 'Happy Christmas, darling, come and see your present.'

'Well,' said I, 'what a surprise,' and we all burst out laughing.

'Come on, in you go.' I had to run back to the house and change. Charlie, who had heroically decided to join me, already had his trunks on. So had Peter.

As my surprise present was now official, I took the opportunity to turn Boxing Day into a swimming party. I rang the Pattersons during the evening. The telephone was answered by Bill. I could hear the wailing of Sally's son in the background. 'Have you had a lovely Christmas Day?' I asked. 'Splendid. William's just caught his finger in his fire engine, otherwise we're all fine. Margaret's gone to bed, and the girls are doing the washing up.' You bet! I thought.

'We've had a lovely day,' I said, 'and we're looking forward to seeing you all tomorrow. What I'm ringing about is to say do please bring bathing things. Just imagine, Charlie's given me a pool-house for Christmas. It's lovely and warm, so I hope you will all enjoy a swim before lunch.'

'Oh yes, I heard about the pool-house. All Littlefold's lost in envy.'

'I'm very lucky, yes,' I said.

'Nice for you, I'm sure. But swimming pools don't add to the value of the property,' said Bill, in his endearing 'more money than sense' tone of voice.

'Come early,' I said. 'It's heated, and there are no draughts. I think a swim would do Margaret good, and she'd enjoy it. She's such a good swimmer, isn't she?'

'Is she?' said Bill.

Somehow Jenny had managed to acquire a very attractive swimming costume, a sleek one-piece, in no way immodest but very flattering to her smooth thighs and pretty bosom. Sally, her own old swimsuit restored to her, lumbered up and down the pool. Even Bill, wearing somewhat lamentable trunks left over from his brave soldiering days, dived in and did a flailing crawl. It was all a great success, with one exception that saddened me.

'You'll swim, Margaret, won't you?' I asked.

'Oh no, thank you so much, Annie, but I'm just not well enough. Maybe one day, when I feel better. But I have so much pain in my shoulder.' There was clearly no point in suggesting that a swim in warm water would help.

Peter took little William by the hand, peeled off his

clothes and carried him, wriggling and squealing into the pool. 'Don't pee all over me,' he said, as William discovered the joy of nakedness in warm water.

'He's sweet with William,' said Margaret.

'You ought to come in,' said Bill. Maybe if Margaret had been a little more devious, she might have taken the opportunity to appear to allow her husband to teach her how to swim. I concluded my own swim, got out and sat with Margaret, chatting inconsequentially.

Jenny swam over to Peter and put her arms round the child. Peter, in return, gave Jenny a friendly hug. 'Everyone out of the pool,' I called, 'it's time for drinks. Let's all go up to the house, and lunch is ready as well.'

'If you'll excuse me,' said Margaret, 'I think I'll just get Jenny to run me home. I really don't feel up to lunch, I'm afraid.'

Charlie had provided excellent wine, and Bill Patterson put away a good share of it.

'It's a shame Margaret couldn't stay,' said Charlie.

'Just as well, I'm afraid,' said Bill. 'She's not much good in company these days. She never was, actually, but lately, she's got worse. I don't know what's the matter with her, she always seems to be in a daze. I can't even get her out of her room to come for even a short walk.'

Jenny spoke up. 'She'll be much better when her shoulder stops hurting and she can come off those pain-killers.'

'I only hope it's as simple as that,' was her father's response.

Sally and her husband had already planned to depart that afternoon. Soon they went off. Bill stayed on, but after a couple of glasses of brandy decided he must go for a good walk and blow away the cobwebs.

Charlie and I eventually decided we were drunk, and had better go to bed. We did so, leaving Peter and Jenny to entertain one another.

Somewhere about half past three in the morning, I heard Jenny's car being started up. It always had a slightly coughing demeanour, I knew it well. Sleepily, I just hoped she could slip into the house unnoticed.

10

Peter left early the next morning. Before he went, he told me that he had, indeed, taken Jenny to bed. 'She wanted to, and I wanted to. She's a little darling. Some bugger had made a balls-up of her first experience, so at least I could put that right.' I let it go at that. A less decent man than Peter would have taken the opportunity right after his London party.

I did not see Jenny for some time after that. I thought perhaps she was feeling shy of me. However, it transpired that she had been busy at home because Colonel Patterson was not well. He had always had a 'gammy leg' which he frequently told us all he never mentioned. It now appeared that he had a problem with the old back, which necessitated lying flat in bed. For a few days, Jenny was waiting on both parents. But then Margaret rallied, and made a courageous effort.

Now that her husband had given up his cooking efforts, she at least had the kitchen to herself and spent hours there cooking meals and snacks.

This resulted, I was happy to see, in Jenny's domestic redundancy. In spite of her previously expressed lack of interest in the Casuarina Tree, she now decided to return to work there, 'for the time being, to earn some money,' was what she said. Dick and Desmond were overjoyed, so much so that they actually came to tell me so.

They telephoned. 'May we come to tea, dear Mrs Finlay?' they asked. 'We've got an afternoon off.'

Although it was a cold day, the wintry sun shone through the glass of our garden room, making it warm enough to have tea there. 'Such heaven,' Desmond flattered endearingly, 'and now do hear about Jenny.'

'Lyons Red Label,' identified Dick, getting his word in. 'Thank goodness. It's all Earl Grey and Green Gunshot at the CT.'

'About Jenny,' Desmond went on, 'she's never looked so bonny. Good for old Colonel P. Flat on his back and keeping Mummy on the run. It's probably done her a power of good too, poor bored soul.'

Dick spread butter and jam on a scone. 'It's not a very good one,' I said, 'I baked them myself. I ought to connect with the W.I., really.'

'It's excellent,' said Dick kindly, and then went on to say, 'apart from the old Col keeping Mrs Col busy, which is why we've got Jenny back. Do you think she's in love? We do.'

'Very likely. It happens,' said Charlie calmly, adding, 'Darling, if tea's finished, what about a little something stronger?'

'We've got to drive,' said Desmond primly.

'Well, said Charlie, 'one of you could drink, surely?'

'All for one, one for all,' said Dick.

'Just like us,' said Charlie.

'In a way,' returned Dick, quite seriously. 'We none of us have children, do we? We love for love's sake.'

I was already anxious about Jenny. Jenny, I knew, was a domestic creature. Her early wish to become an architect had been not so much a big ambition as a love and a feeling for the home-like qualities of four walls and a roof. She cooked. She would want children. However much I hoped that Peter was just a very good experience for her, I couldn't help but wish she had chosen someone nearer her own age and with matrimonial intentions.

She arranged her working hours at the Casuarina Tree to give herself the weekends off. Dick and Desmond, incurably romantic, connived at this system. For her part, Jenny made up by doing very long hours from Monday to Friday.

The early part of the year was cold and grey. I was more and more grateful for my swimming pool-house. Jenny no longer came to swim, but I managed to persuade Charlie that the weight-supported exercise would do his back good. Some of our happiest hours were spent there. There was very little light; a sort of perpetual gloaming. Age fell away from us in that friendly water, and we embraced as though we had eternal youth. Charlie called it our Water Bed.

I put Jenny temporarily out of my mind. I had survived youthful love, and so, I hoped, would she. There was no doubt but that she was spending her weekends with Peter. There was not a thing I could do, so I tried not to think too much about it. I was, perhaps complacently, enjoying my days with Charlie, relishing my swimming pool and congratulating myself that the pleasant life we were leading was well worth having given up a career for.

I looked in on Bill Patterson and suggested that swimming might also be good for his groggy back.

'Might be,' he allowed. 'I'll have to consult the quack.'

'What about Margaret? She might enjoy a swim,' I suggested.

'I don't think so,' he replied. 'She really seems to have ceased to take an interest in anything at all these days. She just about gets out of her room long enough to cook a meal occasionally, but she can't even seem to make much of a fist of that.' I happened to know she was making a great effort in the kitchen, cooking all his meals, but I did not say so. 'I can't even get her to go out for a walk,' he continued, 'so I hardly think she'd come for a swim. In any case, I don't think she's much of a swimmer.'

Again, I kept silent. By now I did believe that Margaret was in the habit of tippling a bit, or maybe a little more than a bit. One day when I called in, I chanced to go into the kitchen. I had spent ten minutes fawning on Bill, a practice I despised in myself but, for Margaret's sake, I had fallen into an attitude of 'anything for a quiet life'.

'I'm just marinading the steak,' said Margaret. She put a few dribbles of red wine on the steak and then swallowed the rest of the glassful rather as though she was the Vicar emptying the Communion cup. After that, and as though it hadn't happened, she offered me a glass of wine and joined me in it. I wondered if the rumours were right and that this was more than her second glass.

She never spoke of Jenny, so I had no idea whether or not she was missing her.

Sally, her husband and her children would appear from time to time for Sunday lunch. I asked Margaret if she was thrilled with having grandchildren. 'I suppose so,' she said vaguely, 'but they are noisy. Still, it's nice for Bill, having grandsons. It was always a sorrow to him that I didn't give him a son. A pity,' she added, I presumed fancifully, 'that Sally wasn't an unmarried mother and then they would have been Pattersons. Poor Bill, his name means so much to him.'

'Any time you'd like a swim, do come over,' I said. 'I go in most days, and sometimes Charlie does, but it makes no difference whether we're there or not. You only have to give the door a shove and it rolls back. Just go in. It would do you good. I've left a couple of towels in there.'

It snowed late in January. I made my way through the sparkling, magical garden to the pool. Charlie announced that he didn't swim while it was snowing. I actually enjoyed going barefoot through the snow, my circulation racing. But the snow didn't last and soon it was wet, windy February. The rain was torrential and the winds violent to gale force.

Margaret, I knew, only went out enough to do the necessary shopping. I felt sorry for her, stuck indoors day in and day out with only Bill Patterson for company. Being stuck indoors all winter is a strain on the happiest couple, so I could imagine that, even with little top-ups in the kitchen, confinement with Bill must be depressing indeed. It was.

It was on a February Sunday that we found Margaret, when we went for our swim, floating face down in the pool.

11

Well, if any month would do it, February came high on the list. I suppose God must have invented February for some reason or another, if only for its black, punitive Old Testament quality.

Over Christmas, and even during the ensuing snow-storms, Charlie and I still cuddled up together and enjoyed it. But in February, eugh! I had reached an age where I did not dare to wish time away. But in February, even I could only long for the whole blasted month to get itself over. And Charlie, normally the most optimistic and equable of men, usually announced, about the middle of the month, that he might not be long for this world.

I couldn't get out into the garden, and I castigated myself for my weary inability to do sensible things in the house, such as cleaning out the attic and throwing out superannuated clothing. But that dismal month rendered me so indecisive that I would pick up a once-favourite sweater, decide it was too tacky for Oxfam, and then put it back in the drawer for fear of hurting its feelings.

I was thankful when I found Margaret, an apparent corpse, that Charlie was with me. I had dragged him down to the pool. 'It will do you good,' I said, getting 'Hrmph' as a reply.

Margaret was not a big woman, but she was fully dressed and waterlogged. How I would have got her out by myself I do not know. Between the two of us, we dragged her on to the pool surround and forced the water out of her. I do not recommend attempting to drown oneself as a means of death. Unless you accomplish your mission, the results are excessively undignified. In a while, Margaret was dribbling snottily, vomiting, peeing and breaking wind.

Charlie, whose country-life activities had included doing a First Aid course, said, 'She may have had a heart attack.' This was the explanation, modified to 'some sort of an attack' that we eventually put about, although the doctor we called out found no evidence of such a thing. Even so, a stay in hospital ensued, which enabled us to make our story believable.

Jenny's toughness during this time astonished me She could see no point in giving up the Casuarina Tree. 'I'm earning money and I need it. It's my life. My father can perfectly well look after himself, and my mother's in hospital, so she's being taken care of.' I had forgotten how self-absorbing being in love is. Whatever the outcome of her passion for Peter, it had certainly had the effect of severing her from her family.

I went to see Margaret. She was in a grimly cheerful ward. 'We have pink blankets here,' she told me. 'I believe there are blue for boys in the next ward. And one of the tea-ladies told me they have green ones as well. Green for gay?' She laughed, but I soon learned that this was but a sad clownishness.

I asked if she was longing to get home. 'No,' she replied. 'It's quite restful here, apart from the silly questions.' What, I enquired, were the silly questions? I thought perhaps someone was trying to find out what ailed this unhappy woman. 'Oh, they want to know if I know what day of the week it is, and do I know the name of the Prime Minister. I longed to say Gladstone.'

'Oh Margaret, they'd think you were barmy, which you're not.'

61

'Aren't I? Anyway, this morning I got my own back. "Do you know the name of the Prime Minister?" the nurse asked. "For heaven's sake, don't you know it yourself, by now? I've told you enough times," I said.'

'Did she laugh?'

'Not her. She just said she'd only just come on duty.'

It was patently clear that Margaret was occupying a bed too many. She was repeatedly told how much better a recovery she would make in her own home.

There was no apparent reason why she should fall out of bed, re-damage her shoulder and break her wrist again. Sister was not best pleased. 'It's not as though she had a stroke. She's well under sixty and perfectly healthy.' I felt that Sister was only just restraining herself from adding 'sheer tiresomeness'.

Margaret, once again encased in plaster, had to be found somewhere in the hospital to stay. I found her in a ward where her companions all appeared to be demented or else in extremis. It was so ghastly that I hoped she would believe it better to go home than to stay longer. But she just seemed to close her eyes and her mind to her surroundings.

I was pleased to see that Jenny, at this stage, was compassionate enough to pay frequent visits.

I rang Sally, risking the interference, ostensibly pretending that I thought she might not know that her mother was still in the hospital.

'Thank you so much. And thank you for going to see her. I'm sure it does her a great deal of good. I might try and go, but it's terribly difficult. I can't leave the children, and I really don't want them to see their darling Granny all ill and funny.'

Margaret spoke with the nearest thing I saw in her to happiness of Jenny's visits. 'She's looking so pretty,' she said.

'She's enjoying working again,' I replied. 'She really loves it at the Casuarina Tree, and they think the world of her there.'

Margaret said, 'She goes to London quite often, at weekends. I'm glad of it. She hasn't had much fun for a while, and it obviously does her good to get away from Littlefold. I'm glad she has friends in town.' We left the conversation at that shallow level.

I was present on the day when Margaret's husband came to visit. It so happened that Jenny had come, and for once had persuaded Sally to join her. I had stepped outside to leave the two daughters alone with their mother for a little while. Thus I was beside the desk, with its assemblage of doctors and nurses, when Bill appeared.

One of the doctors, who looked as though he could do with a day in bed, heard Bill say to the sister, 'Colonel Patterson, to see Mrs Patterson.'

'You're her husband, are you?' the doctor asked. Bill nodded. The doctor continued, 'I'd like a word. You see, we don't really feel it's doing her a lot of good, remaining here. She's among very sick people, and although she has injuries that must mend, there's really very little we can do for her as an in-patient. I could arrange for her to visit the physiotherapist, but I'm quite certain she would be better off at home with a loving family.'

'I see,' said Bill. 'Get the patients out, shorten the waiting list.'

I pretended to be reading a notice telling patients their rights. I could safely keep my back turned as it was hidden away where no patient could possibly see it.

'We are indeed very stretched,' said the doctor civilly, 'but I do assure you that we don't turn patients out if they'd be better off here.'

Bill now decided, I could hear from my listening point, to throw himself on the doctor's mercy. 'You see, doctor, the problem is this. You say "a loving family". True, but our daughters are grown up and gone, and I'm not as strong as I was. I have old injuries, you understand. I'm very lame, alas. If she should fall, I don't know how I would manage.'

'Is she apt to fall?' asked the doctor. 'Has that happened frequently?'

I turned to see Bill nodding, this time conveying bravely concealed sorrow and weariness as he said, 'Well, I'll try to do my best.'

'Don't worry too much at the moment. We'll keep her for a couple more days,' was his reward.

'That's very good of you. I do see you chaps are doing all you can in difficult conditions.'

I chose this moment to slip away and go home to Charlie. 'I'm sort of sorry for Bill Patterson in a way, even though I don't like him,' I said to him. 'The poor man's bewildered.'

'Is he?' asked Charlie.

'I suppose it's army life, but he really doesn't know anything about Margaret. I don't consider I know much about her myself, but I certainly seem to know more about her than he does. For one thing, I know a woman who tried to drown herself.'

Almost any married couple in the world must be closer than were Bill and Margaret.

Even though I had completely recovered from, and rejected my previous life by the time I joined forces with Charlie, I've always known he knows of it, simply as a part of knowing and loving me. He, when I married him, still had a mistress, but she drifted away. She was a well-mannered woman who had the grace to avoid getting to know me.

I grew up in a neighbourhood much like Littlefold. There were some aspects of my life which were a little like

64

Jenny's, although my mother and father were very different from Margaret and Bill Patterson. *My* only difficulty in getting away from home was that they adored me and entertained for me. My mother longed to re-create the pre-war atmosphere in which she had herself grown up.

During the war she kept hens, did more than her fair share for canteens, care of evacuees, collecting salvage and fund-raising. She also did without any domestic help, and made clothes for me. Our war was very much a home-front war. I was under six when it began. My father, who was a few years older than my mother, ran the local Home Guard.

After the war, we all settled down to trying to give dinner parties. Rationing went on and on. To this day, if anyone says 'carrot cake' or 'rhubarb and date jam' to me, I still heave. But we were getting better off for clothes. I was too young to wear the New Look, but longed for it. As soon as I could, I had bouncy skirts tightly belted below a white school blouse with the top two buttons undone. I was, I believe, quite a popular local girl.

It was from this safe haven that I launched myself on London. In wartime there had been an influx of all classes of servicemen and women, not to mention quite a few of different races. But now, as no doubt Littlefold was also doing at the same time, my neighbourhood dedicated itself to returning to some semblance of normality as quickly as possible.

When I was twenty, I had a brief affair with the son of some acquaintances of my mother and father. He was a good deal older than me, and had served in India and Burma during the war. Whatever experiences he had had in India, they had not included the discovery of the Kama Sutra. He was not an adventurous lover, and it was to be some time before I discovered the orgasm.

His name was Jeremy and he wanted to marry me.

According to Jeremy, I was right for him in every way. For a while, I was an engaged girl. Though not as glamorous in tweeds as he no doubt had been in uniform, he was still very good looking and I was awed by being the chosen bride of an older man. I acted (largely for my own benefit) the part of a blissful girl in love. In a way, I wanted to be married. Even in my schooldays, the main competition had been who would get married the soonest.

I don't remember actually making up my mind to quit, or the exact moment when I did it. I know I picked a quarrel. Jeremy was the son of a lawyer, already into partnership, and a sought-after catch. I knew that many girls in the neighbourhood had their eyes on him, and I pretended to be jealous of one of them. There wasn't the slightest reason for this, but it caused Jeremy to become nervous of my 'possessiveness', so in the end I don't think he was too sorry to be rid of me.

I shed a few tears for form's sake, and went to London. To seek my fortune?

12

I knew my mother was disappointed that I refused to have a 21st birthday party. I made light of it. 'How about a broken-engagement party?' I suggested.

'Oh darling, we all thought you were so happy. You and Jeremy seemed so well-suited?'

'Did you like him?'

'That's not really the point,' said my ever-reasonable mother. 'We just wanted you to be happy.'

I knew this to be true, so I replied evasively, 'Well, who knows? Maybe a bit of a break will do us both good.'

I had no idea what I was going to do when I got to London, but it wasn't very difficult for a girl to get a job at that time, especially if she didn't mind a humble level, and humble levels were what most girls then, including me, expected. For several years after the war, the returning men constantly competed for the jobs of aspiration, so a reasonably attractive, well-spoken girl could always pick up what was left over at the tail end.

Also, it was amazingly easy (Jenny was astonished when I told her this, years later) to get quite cheap digs in Chelsea or Kensington. Mind you, I'm talking about a bed-sitter with a lumpy divan that served as both bed and sofa, a broken pre-war Lloyd Loom chair, bleak lighting, a minute greasy cooker in the corner, an unsavoury bathroom with a lethal geyser, shared between the whole house, and one loo on the landing. The bath was cast iron with a permanent rust stain below the taps, and there was usually a string of damp stockings, knickers and petticoats to slap you in the face as you got into it.

Although several of the bed-sitterees were male, I seldom noticed any of their underwear or socks on the washing line. Judging by the smell on the landing, I imagine their washing waited until they went home to Mum.

The basement of the house was occupied by the owner's son. It was, by origin, quite a grand house. Being in a heavily bombed area, it had become valueless during the war, and the owners had moved away and let it deteriorate into a quick turnover renting deal. It is now worth countless millions.

To put my mother's mind at rest, I started my London life in a hostel, the YWCA to be precise. From there I went forth in search of a job. I did a lot of walking, until one day I found myself in Sloane Square. I very much liked what I saw in the windows of Peter Jones, but I liked much better what I saw in the windows of WH Smith. Books.

I was determined to manage on my own. Apart from anything else I had blown it with Jeremy, not that I cared about that.

Luckily WH Smith needed an assistant. I claimed matric level in Eng Lit. It was as well I didn't claim a degree, as WH Smith's wages policy didn't cater for demanding graduates. I think I got about £3 a week and I imagine the young men got at least fifteen shillings more.

The YWCA cost thirty shillings a week with breakfast and supper. By going without lunch, I could just about manage the bus fares, stockings and some make-up. Then I found out how to get rid of the bus fares. Grete, a rather dodgy 27-year-old divorcee, whom I couldn't help admiring, had digs 'just round the corner, darling. Très chic address, très chambres primitifs.' Thus I galloped to my fate.

The name Davidson did not signify anything to me. One of my school friends was called Anita Davidson and her father was a Canon of the Church of England. Jack Davidson was blue-eyed with corn-coloured curly hair.

When I first met Jack, short, as I subsequently learnt, for Jacob, he was a couple of years down from Cambridge. He had achieved a First. The world was his oyster but as he hadn't yet found the pearl in it, his indulgent mother had persuaded his father to let him run the town house and its tenants until such time as she could get it returned to its former glory.

The sudden but complete demise of my horrid little electric cooker left me supperless on a Thursday evening. On the day before pay day there was no hope of taking myself out to a meal, even at the three and threepence charged by the Cinderella Cafe for a choice of stewed whale-meat or spam fritters, potatoes and carrots with steamed sponge pudding to follow; coffee threepence extra.

The basement had once been kitchen, scullery, butler's pantry and still room. The huge kitchen was now converted by Jack as a sitting room. It was cosy, in a louche manner. Jack, the chronic undergraduate, had filled it with sybaritic seating arrangements, colourful silks and Edwardian lamps. To me, brought up in a world of chintz, gate-legged tables and open windows, this was totally captivating.

It was also the first time I had ever seen a shirt made of wool taffeta, and the first time I had ever seen a man wearing rose-coloured linen trousers. There was nothing in the least effeminate about Jack. Heavens, no! He just happened to like gorgeous fabrics. I was soon to learn the meaning of the word 'tactile'.

Somewhat overwhelmed by all this stylishness, I snapped abruptly, 'My rotten little cooker has packed up, and I can't make my supper unless you fix it for me right away.'

'Fix it? Me?'

'I thought you were in charge.'

'I am, darling, but I'm not an electrician.'

'Well,' I said firmly, 'get one then. I can't cook my supper, and I can't go out because I don't get paid until tomorrow.'

'That at least we can solve. Why not take a glass of this delicious hock? No seltzer, I'm afraid, Oscar Wilde I am not. I'm no cook, either, so the only way I can feed you is to take you out.' I had never been to Soho before, and I had thought all Italian food was spaghetti, which I had only eaten out of a tin, heated in a pan on my little cooker.

I had, at home, after one triumphant visit on my mother's part to the butcher, eaten roast veal. But I had never eaten osso bucco. I had, when the hens at the bottom of our garden did well, eaten egg custard, but I had never tasted zabaglione.

I had experienced a form of sexual intercourse, but not a *coup de foudre*.

When Jenny's passion for Peter Baker was taking its inexorable course, I refrained from ever mentioning my own past. She thought of me as a wise friend who had only and ever been married to Charlie Finlay. And apart from all that, I knew I would have died of embarrassment myself if, at Jenny's age, some old lady, no matter how fond I might have been of her, had started telling me about her long-ago blazing love affair.

I had not really forgotten it altogether. It was just that the past had been put in its place by very much better subsequent events. I did take a degree of pride in that I had fought my way out of all that happened between me and Jack well before I came together with Charlie. After Jack deserted me, I was so lonely and desperate that I went out with any man who asked me. On a couple of occasions, I very nearly got married. But by great good fortune, my career prospects, to my surprise, improved. So as my love life got worse, my finances got better and I was spared having to grasp at any old marriage in the storm. The one thing I had, in the end, to thank Jack for was that while I was high on love for him, my confidence had become such that I had walked straight and easily into my first job in the advertising business.

To go back to Jack. He and I were very soon sleeping together, ecstatically, sometimes in his basement quarters, sometimes on my narrow divan bed. Jack loved me, it seemed, quite as passionately as I loved him. Very soon I was to feel a sense of permanence, because he insisted on taking me to be fixed up with a diaphragm.

The happiness I experienced at that time did wonders for my self-esteem. I was loved and, better still, I was allowed to give love. Jack enjoyed being adored. This gave me the feeling that I could achieve anything.

I was aware that Jack, in his capacity of what was called 'running the house', was really and truly as yet without a job. I had no intention of allowing him to do just any old thing and ruin his chances of greatness. So that was when I decided to go into advertising, and was quite soon taken on as a junior copywriter by a firm called SH Crayton. This company had been founded at the beginning of the First World War, and its proprietor, Samuel Henry had, of necessity, promoted women to board level. To his eternal credit he was loyal enough to those women that they remained in their positions forever, and set a precedent. I became one of their post-World War Two descendants. I have always been glad that Samuel Henry became a knight.

Jack and I were lying sated in each other's arms early one morning when he suddenly said, in an unusually serious voice, 'There's something you have to know about me.' I was greatly relieved when it turned out not to be that he had acquired a secret wife in his university days. It seemed simple when he went on to say, 'I am a Jew.'

'What does that matter? It makes no difference to me,' I said, imagining that his concern was that my conventional C of E family would object to my marrying a Jew. I knew nothing, at that time, about what it meant, and frequently still does mean, to be Jewish. Quite simply, if Jack were to marry me, it would mean a defiance that would result in his being disinherited. He told me how much he loved me, and how it would break his heart to lose me.

I knew very little about great wealth. My own family was comfortably off. We lived in a nice old house, rather like the one Charlie and I live in now. But the Davidsons, I learnt, owned very large amounts of property, not only the London house but also around coastal areas which were becoming more and more popular and profitable now that all threat of invasion was well over. Jack's father had bought cleverly. He and his wife were both long-descended Orthodox Jews, and she was deeply involved with Hadassah, and active in Jewish charities. Her way of life was of prime importance to her. A non-Jewish daughter-in-law would be out of the question.

Jack knew about Jeremy. He knew because I had told him often that I had never known what making love meant until now. 'Why didn't you marry Jeremy?' he would ask when wanting to be complimented on his prowess.

'You know quite well why,' I would reply when I could get enough breath.

I could, I thought, understand what being cut off without a shilling meant to Jack. He would be unable to support me, the girl he loved. 'But,' I said, 'we could make it on our own. I have a good job. I'm earning lots of

72

money.' Twelve hundred pounds a year was untold wealth to me at that time. I added, 'And once you get started, we'll be well away.'

I longed with all my heart to be married to Jack, for love of him and for the need of being acknowledged as his wife, free and open to take him home. I thought perhaps that one day his parents would come to see that I was the right woman for him. I thought they might accept that wealth meant nothing to me, and that I was ready to earn for both of us if necessary. Surely a Jewish family that had accrued wealth throughout years of application would come to appreciate a daughter-in-law who could do the same? I had a hard lesson to learn.

The only way I could keep Jack was to go on as things were. I had to accept that in the hope that there would be 'one day'. For now happiness (bliss, in fact) was to be in Jack's arms.

I seldom went home, because Jack, no doubt all too aware of the future, would not come with me. This neglect hurt my mother and father, but I was as selfish as only a girl desperately in love can be.

I was only really miserable when Jack went home to his parents, naturally without taking me. I imagined (with reason) his mother lining up suitable Jewish girls for him. Occasionally Jack would feel guilty about me, but I clung on for two years. I tried never to whinge. Jack liked to laugh in bed, and he liked me to laugh with him.

What happened next was not intended. I was punctilious about taking care. Desperately though I longed to be Jack's wife, I would never have resorted to trickery. I truly hoped that one day his parents might soften towards me, and the last thing I would ever have done would have been to give them a chance to blame him for getting into the clutches of a schemer.

Furthermore, I had no wish to give up my job. At least

I was no financial burden, and I loved what I was doing. I loved the trade I had adopted. We in advertising rather proudly referred to it as a trade and not a profession. I did not intend to become pregnant.

Much as I relished the passion of Jack's love-making, I always found a particular sweetness in his consideration of me when I had a period. He would pet and stroke me, and direct jokes at his own member. 'You may look but don't touch. The missis has a tummy-ache.' Being called 'the missis' was my greatest comfort.

I had renewed my diaphragm recently. Did I buy a dud? It was difficult enough in those days for an unmarried young woman to get birth control help. The Marie Stopes clinic wouldn't let you through the door. So you went to whatever quack would take your money.

Well, whatever happened, it happened. And by the time two months had gone by, I knew I desperately wanted this baby of Jack's. When it began, Jack noticed it almost before I did. He was always as aware of the cycles of my body as I was myself. 'Aren't you about due for the curse?' he asked, in bed. I replied only vaguely, as I felt like making love.

A few days further on, Jack said, 'It's getting a bit late, isn't it? Are you sure you're all right?'

Mother Nature is a curious creature. I had no intention of trapping Jack, but every muscle of my body began to cling to what was inside it.

At the advertising agency in which I worked, women's lives were far more advanced than elsewhere. My own group-head was a woman with two small children. She was the salient earner in her marriage. Her husband was the proprietor of a rather unfortunate picture-gallery too far from Chelsea and too far into Fulham. He had been on the Burma railroad. My boss was, necessarily, highly organised. She left the house at eight each morning, and woe betide the daily nanny if she was not there on time.

I dreamed and planned. I did not realise the awfulness of what Jack would suggest. He did, according to his lights, his best. He sought, once the pregnancy was definite, a solution, one that shattered me. It was that I should return home, butter up my ex-fiancé Jeremy, and marry him. 'But it's *your* baby,' I howled, 'that's why I love it.'

'But you know I can't marry you. I would be penniless if I did.'

'But I work. I work with other women who manage to have children and keep their jobs. And you could work. For God's sake, Jack, you could bloody well work. What's wrong with you getting a job? You've got a First. You could get anything, instead of playing at managing this house.'

'It would kill my mother,' he said, finalising the disaster ahead.

I was just over three months pregnant when I had the abortion. I had nowhere to go except back to the doctor who had supplied the dud cap. He mucked up my hope of child-bearing, once and for all, although I did not know that at the time. I only knew that my heart was broken. Jack had given me a little Victorian silver brooch. It had a weak pin to hold it, but it was pretty with forget-me-nots and ANNIE inscribed on it. I had been very ill and lost a great deal of blood. I threw the brooch at Jack as I left. 'It was made for a housemaid. Perhaps you might have treated a housemaid better.' I was briefly elated by being dramatic. But not for long.

13

All that was a very long time ago. After we broke up (I put it that way at the time to save my pride from having to admit that Jack had deserted me) I moved out. This was only because I had no alternative. I could hardly go on living in a house belonging to Jack's father and mother. Fortunately I could afford a flat of my own, a small one over a shoe-repair shop.

I was half-mad with misery, but somehow I managed to do my job well enough that at least I didn't get fired. Jessie, my boss, merely assumed that I had been dieting, so thin did I become.

I can hardly remember the names of the men I went out with at that time. I drank a good deal, it was the only way I could bear the company I was keeping. Once I even accepted a proposal of marriage only to wake up next morning to the shaming realisation that I hadn't the faintest idea who it was that had proposed.

However, at last sanity began to set in. My twenties were rapidly passing, and the grim prospect of being thirty and still single stared me in the face. I made what I still know was a brave decision. It was that I would brace myself to remain single, rather than marry just for the sake of being called Mrs. The face of this was bleak. If I was known to have experienced the life I had had with Jack, I was a scarlet woman. Otherwise, I had to appear as a spinster, a seemingly rejected, inexperienced virgin. Well, I weathered it.

All my school friends were married, and I, as a well-salaried advertising lady, was in much demand as a god-mother. Then, just as I had genuinely resigned myself to a lifetime on my own, darling Charlie came my way. It is almost impossible to explain the beginning of my love for him and his for me.

I had been married to him for three or four months when I got an unexpected telephone call. 'Annie?'

I couldn't fail to recognise the voice. 'Yes,' I said cautiously.

'I've been thinking about you. I miss you.'

'I once missed you,' I said.

'What about having lunch with me. Osso bucco? Zabaglione?'

'Jack, I am married.'

'I know you are. So am I,' he replied.

'I trust to a suitable Jewish girl.'

'Yes. She's very nice. But I miss you. Please come and have lunch with me, at least.'

'No,' I said. I was not to be tempted, and I had no wish to be tormented.

It was remarkable enough that I had had the good fortune to be loved by Charlie after the messy wilderness years I had been through. It would never have happened if I had not concentrated so hard on the career that then looked like becoming my whole life.

There were salient changes coming in at Crayton's. Commercial TV, to be precise. Up until then, magazines and newspapers had been the mainstay. Elegant and sometimes witty copy had been worth the effort to write. This era was a gracious one that now appears about on a par with dancing a pavane. We all wrote our copy in longhand and the department secretary typed it up for us, religiously honouring every verb, pronoun and comma.

Commercial TV came as a shock at the time, not to be equalled until the much later arrival of the internet.

Many of the older women left to live on their pensions in small houses in Sevenoaks and Seaford and so on. But I had no alternative but to remain. I could have moved to another agency, but having no television experience I would have been hard put to it to match my salary.

Suddenly my dignified playground was filled with rough boys. It was Girls Out Of The Sandpit. TV with its technicalities was men's work. The woman executive with whom I had been agreeably working for years disappeared to be replaced by a man called Charles Finlay.

My first experience of Charlie was that he was impressive. So impressive and so sure of himself that he was able to speak to the likes of me with what I regarded as a patronising pretence of humility. 'I don't know the first thing about this TV stuff!' What he did know, however, was how to get hold of the right in-house producers, the right storyboard makers and the right outside production companies. The clients, of course, adored him. Charlie exuded understated authority.

He had at that time a beautiful mistress who used to call for him at the agency, sometimes at the close of day, and not infrequently at lunchtime as well.

I hardly knew him and he hardly knew me. So it came as a considerable surprise when he asked me to utilise one of the ideas I had been developing for old-fashioned newsprint for a TV commercial. 'Who, me?' I asked sharply. 'Surely one of the lads should be doing that.'

'It's a cosmetic account, it needs a woman. And, I might add, the lads, as you call them, don't exactly have your way with words.'

It was only after Charlie and I were married that he told me he had fancied me from the first day he set foot in the agency.

We were married in church. Charlie had, up until then, evaded the knot, and the knot had evaded me. So off we went to St Luke's. The marriage certificate gives Charles John Finlay as advertising executive and Ann Mary Sefton as spinster.

With very few exceptions, couples who got married were not allowed to stay in the same agency. And it was pretty nearly always the wife who left, equality not yet having got that far. In my case, I left to join an up-coming shop called Welbeck, Tannhauser and Streem. It was there that Jack traced me. Charlie told me later that an old friend had been trying to contact me at Crayton's and had been put through to him. So Charlie had unwittingly opened the door to my ex-lover. I had closed it long ago, and now I closed it again, once and for all.

It was only a year before Jenny met Peter that I saw Jack one more time. I had been a little unwell, and Charlie had persuaded me to go to London and see the doctor who had looked after me in my yuppy days. Who should be in the waiting room but a white-haired, testy-faced old man whom I recognised with difficulty as the young lover who had once held me in thrall. He seemed to be suffering from nothing worse than a bad cold but was as furious about being kept waiting as though he was in the throes of a heart attack. It was very easy to walk away.

There were other reasons to eschew backward thinking. Events in Littlefold.

I had no intention of becoming deeply involved with Margaret Patterson. It was Jenny who interested me, Jenny of whom I had become so fond. Long before my friend Peter came into her life, I had liked the way she tackled working in our garden, and I had admired the resolution with which she left her stupid job at the Estate Agents, and had the courage to become a waitress.

I had become aware that now I hardly ever saw Margaret,

even though spring was allegedly coming in. Bill Patterson was frequently seen about the village, working at being popular. It has never been difficult to be popular in Littlefold. Charlie was well liked because he was genuinely kind and completely unself-seeking I also was reasonably well liked. But Bill Patterson made himself forcefully likeable, reactionary, right-wing and a Blair-loather. Bill was resolutely backward-looking, which suited Littlefold to a T.

I often saw him with a woman called Tess Simpson. Charlie found this intensely amusing. 'Do you think he's bonking her?' he asked.

'Are you mad?' I replied. 'Can you imagine any woman in her right mind wishing to be bonked by Bill Patterson?'

'Well, Margaret was, dearie. There are two children to prove it.'

The general consensus in Littlefold was that Bill Patterson was a man to be pitied. Littlefold is always rumour-rife. So Jenny, working as a common waitress, was sure to have undesirable friends. Dick and Desmond said to me, 'Undesirable? Us? We're a mother to Jenny. Poor child, her own mother can't do much for her. She's very weird, isn't she?'

I had no idea what to say to this. Something in me wanted to spring to Margaret's defence but I didn't know how to do it, since Margaret had not only fallen downstairs in unexplained circumstance but also, to my certain knowledge, tried to drown herself in our pool.

I began to think that however hopeless her love for Peter might be, it was a better option for Jenny than what she had at home.

Bill Patterson dined out. Margaret was never well enough to go out to dinner. And a spare man (even one like Bill Patterson) at table is always welcome in Littlefold, with its preponderance of widows, not to mention visiting female divorcees, relicts and spinsters. He was not invited to our house. Charlie, who had left advertising for a peaceful life, and was anyway a man of peace, merely regarded him as a crashing bore. 'If you're going to cook nice things, let's at least feed people who are a bit amusing.'

New arrivals were a blood-transfusion in Littlefold. Tess and Bernard Simpson, who had thought the outskirts of Sevenoaks were country living, happened to drive through Littlefold one day. 'Heaven! And so near the sea,' they cried, and bought Wisteria Cottage. They involved themselves rapidly, and knew how to behave. They resolutely refrained from complaining about the late arrival of newspapers, the badgers which tore up their garden, and the length of time it took to buy a chicken and a pound of potatoes in the village shop. It had taken me a good while to understand that this meeting-ground was a lifeline for elderly, carless villagers.

The Simpsons homed in straight away on Colonel Patterson. They were only in their mid-fifties, but had taken early retirement. They were quite likeable, in their way. Tess was keen on starting a writing group, or a painting group or some such thing. She very kindly invited me to take up one of these activities.

'Bill Patterson is very keen,' she said. 'He started to do tapestry but he had to give it up when his wife became so unwell.'

That his wife had tried to drown herself in my swimming pool I did not mention. That episode had the knock-on effect that now, unless Charlie could be dragged into the pool, I swam by myself. It hardly seemed quite the thing to invite a woman to return to the scene at which she had attempted to do herself in.

Tess Simpson was not a malicious woman, merely a rather foolish one. She dropped me a few heavily loaded hints, such as that poor Bill Patterson's wife was on the bottle. I had slightly thought that myself, but now I said resolutely, 'Absolute nonsense. Who told you such a thing?'

March had come in with its usual deceptive behaviour, pretending that spring was on the way. The grass began to grow, and Charlie started once again to do wheelies on the sit-on mower. Primroses began to appear but they seemed to be scentless. I felt old; I had been able to smell them when I was a child. I went to the dentist. I always shore up my teeth. I can't think of anything more humiliating than mumbling in a hospital ward through an empty mouth. Gloomy? Yes.

I intended to go and see Margaret. I felt perpetually guilty about not going, especially as Margaret was more commented upon than visited at that time.

I saw Jenny once or twice, at the Casuarina Tree. She smiled, served my lunch, and retreated behind Dick and Desmond.

'How is your mother?' I asked.

'Fine, thanks,' said Jenny.

'And you?'

'Fine, thanks.'

No more was said.

Ever since we first came to Littlefold, Charlie and I had resisted the temptation to own pets. We argued that we might as well benefit from the freedom from responsibility which our childless state gave us.

I had had a charming dog when I was little. Even so I was the first to say, 'No animals. No ties. That means we can always go off on our travels whenever we please.'

Charlie thought this was quite funny, since I, once I had overcome my reluctance to leave my London life and my business travelling, rapidly became the one who made the most excuses for never going away.

However, towards the end of March, my old boss Jessie, long retired and now a widow, developed gall-bladder trouble and so had to go into hospital to have the offending organ removed. She rang to tell me about this and said, 'It's really nothing to worry about. I'll be better than new in a few weeks. But Annie, my real worry is Fang.'

Fang, I happened to know, was a Pekingese. An odd name for a small dog which had more halitosis than teeth. My own childhood friend had been a large, amenable, greedy Labrador.

When Fang arrived, which, of course, he did (in fact Charlie actually drove straight up to Jessie's flat in St John's Wood to collect him), I was appalled. Unlike the late Prince (my mother had had the greatest difficulty in obtaining sufficient red meat, during the war, to satisfy his appetite), Fang, small, testy and miserable without Jessie, declared all food to be filth. 'An anorexic peke,' I wailed. 'Just my luck.'

All this time, I had been bracing myself to go and see poor Margaret. Then on a day when I was scouring the village shop to find some delicacy the wretched animal would eat, who should be there but Margaret. As usual, conversation was buzzing about as people discussed the cholesterol content of biscuits, and the state of their hearts and hips. 'Margaret,' I said, 'how are you? I haven't seen you for such a long time.'

'I haven't been very well,' she replied.

Just to chat, I said, 'I'm looking for something a pernickety peke will eat.'

'I didn't know you had a dog.'

'Neither have I, really. It's only for a while. An old friend of mine is ill and I'm looking after her little dog. I've tried everything, chicken, turkey, duck, a boiled egg. Not a bite.'

'You're underestimating the dog. He probably needs exercise more than anything.'

Thus it was that Margaret Patterson and I began to go for walks with Fang. I was as surprised by her perception of a little dog's needs as I had been by her ability to swim like a fish.

There were many pleasant footpaths around Littlefold. One of these, fortunately, began at the end of our garden, so we could get straight onto it. Walking in the actual lanes and roads had become a life-threatening exercise, between lorries, aggressive cyclists and what Charlie calls the boy-racerists.

Much to my surprise, Margaret appeared in gumboots. 'They're Sally's, actually, from when she was a girl. She goes in for green wellies now.' I also learnt that she had no qualms about Jenny working at the Casuarina Tree. 'Bill hates it. He can't see how much she loathed working at the estate agent's. In any case, I have a suspicion that something unpleasant happened to her there. She's very much happier now.' She went on then to say, 'She goes to London at weekends quite often, you know. I don't ask her much about it, but I'm pretty sure she's seeing your very nice friend Peter. I rather hope she is.'

'He's a lot older than she is, and also divorced,' I told her.

'So what?' said Margaret.

Fang took a great fancy to her, and demanded that she throw sticks for him and then fetch them back herself. She always came back to our house after walks, and it was she who put Fang into the kitchen sink and washed the clots of mud from between the sensitive pads of his feet.

It was difficult to equate this person with the crazy recluse she was seen as by many people in Littlefold. It came clearly to my mind that Margaret Patterson was a deeply sane woman.

14

It was about this time that Jenny began to open up with me about Peter.

Early in April, an elderly cousin of Charlie's died, and he asked me to go with him to the funeral. This involved driving to Shropshire, so we decided to stay over for a night. As the old gentleman had been somewhat formal, I dug out a now disused black business coat and skirt, and Charlie bought a new black tie. So we packed up our suitable accoutrements of woe, asked Margaret to take care of Fang for a couple of days, and off we went.

As the cousin was ninety, and his surviving wife eighty nine, we at least had the benefit of being the young things at the obsequies.

We got home on a Thursday evening. I rang to tell Margaret, and to offer to go and fetch Fang. Jenny, answering the telephone said, 'I'm not working this evening, so I'll bring him.'

We needed to unwind. It had been a trying drive on the return journey, and Charlie's back was hurting him. I wanted him to get into the swimming pool, but his response was that the therapy he most required was a large whisky, the return of Fang, although he usually swore he couldn't stand the little monster, and a sight of pretty Jenny.

Curiously enough, it was Charlie who inadvertently opened the dam. He is not a man to ask questions. As he says, 'Don't ever ask anyone around here how they are. They'll tell you, and it will take two hours.'

On this occasion, he took Fang onto his lap and played with his charming ears, having first suggested to Jenny that she might like a glass of wine. As I knew my tired husband would need at least one more large whisky, I went into the kitchen and brought out snacks of bread, salami and Cheddar cheese.

I do not advocate drunkenness, but there are times when a little of it is a good idea. After the second glass of Chardonnay, Jenny looked at Charlie, who was looking at her over the silky head of the Pekingese, and said, 'I'm thinking of changing my way of life.' Actually, she said 'lifestyle' but I forgave her as I wanted to hear what was coming next.

'Giving up the Casuarina Tree?' I asked, thinking that that would at least please her father.

'Yes. But I'm not giving up doing food. In fact, what I want to do is business lunches. Oh, it's all right, I don't think I know it all. But I think I can apprentice myself to someone who's doing it now. I'd be dogsbody, but I'd learn. This woman's in the City. It's a very profitable business.' Jenny now began to speak very fast, even though with affected nonchalance. 'She's an old friend of Peter Baker's, you see. I wouldn't be earning much at first, but I could stay at Peter's place. He's got plenty of room.'

'But Jenny,' I had to say, 'do you think that's wise?'

'Oh, I know it was different in your day, Annie,' she said, thus linguistically putting me in my elderly place. 'But it doesn't mean anything these days. Everyone shares unisex. It doesn't mean they're sleeping together.'

After Jenny had gone, Charlie said sardonically, 'Want to bet?'

I was trying to decide, while walking with Margaret, whether to bring up the subject of Jenny, and my fears for her, when Fang kindly created a diversion. His libido apparently enhanced by his much improved appetite, Fang now fell in love. The object of his affections was a lady pug twice his size. They kissed, flat nose to flat nose, although little Fang had to stand on his hind legs.

Margaret laughed more heartily than I had ever heard before. 'Well,' she said, holding her sides, 'at least they'd both snore in bed. It would be better than some marriages.' She further added, 'I had the Jehovah's Witnesses round last week. So I told them, "Not me, thanks, but there's a Chinese character up the road who might like to see you." I didn't say where, you'll be glad to know.'

It was awfully difficult to know about Margaret. Whatever the case, we walked home with nothing said between us about Jenny.

However, it was from Margaret that I learnt when Jenny left home and went to London. 'I'm glad she has,' she said. 'I've no real idea what she's doing, but I do know it's better for her than being here.'

'Are you unhappy here, Margaret?' I naturally had to ask.

'No. Not really. I made my bed, as they say. And I do have a home. Poor Bill,' she added, I thought somewhat elliptically.

It was some time until I saw Jenny again. She came down for a weekend in May, to see her mother. She was on her own. I heard from Margaret that she was coming. 'May I suggest that she comes over to you for a swim?' she said.

Charlie and I were both pleased to see our young friend. Jenny talked as she swam. Under the champagney influence of the water, her previous smoke-screen disappeared. It was 'Peter this' and 'Peter says' and 'We' all the time. We, it seemed, had had people to dinner and Jenny had cooked guineafowl my way.

We joined Charlie, who was enjoying his Saturday Guinness. 'How's the project going?' he asked.

'The project?'

'Yes. The business lunch enterprise? How is it going?'

'Oh. Yes. Very well, thank you. I'm learning a lot.'

I joined in at this point. 'Jenny,' I said, 'it will be really good for you to have your own business eventually.'

'Yes,' said Jenny. She lifted Fang off Charlie's lap and buried her face in the soft place above his flat little nose.

15

Summer came in, and turned out to be the summer in which I was glad still to have decent legs. Owning a swimming pool has always been an instant passport to social desirability, and we were now rather more popular than I could have wished.

Among others, Sally (née Patterson) quite frequently brought her two little boys. A swim fitted in nicely before Sunday lunch at her parents'. She regarded it as a treat for me; she was that sort of mother. They were not bad kids, certainly rather more likeable than their mother. It pleased Bill Patterson that they were made welcome by Charlie and me, and pleasing Bill Patterson became a necessary chore. I had come to enjoy my walks with Margaret more and more, and I had the pleasure of believing that my company actually did her some good. Fang served an excellent purpose.

However, his visit was soon to come to an end. My old friend Jessie came down for a few days recuperation and reintroduction to her little dog. Fang greeted her with courtesy. The few days of Jessie's visit were reasonably pleasant, although she was prone to reminiscences of people who had actually been far senior to me in my early advertising days. It felt like the first and second world wars running together in historical memory. Jessie was a good ten or twelve years older than me, but she continually spoke of 'us' and 'in our day'. I hadn't the heart to point out that her contemporaries were not mine, but I did begin to find it rather depressing.

By the time Jessie and Fang departed, I found myself looking to see if my ankles had swollen, and clutching at my heart for atrial fibrillation. Even Charlie began to refer to infectious geriatry, and had to be cuddled back to reality.

Tess Simpson made another contribution to my sense of decrepitude. I had hardly shaken off Jessie's equation of my age with her own when Tess started in with kindly advice. I caught a slight summer cold, and Tess warned me to take care, come winter. 'Be sure and get your flu jab,' she said. 'I've insisted that my mother and father have them.'

'I don't think I'll bother,' I replied quippingly, 'I'll just wrap up in my shawl and put a piece of red flannel on my chest.' With equal kindness, Tess now explained to me that red flannel was an old wives' tale.

At this point, Charlie started to go on about making our wills. I knew he was only being businesslike but it was still a depressing exercise I could have done without.

Much as I loathe leaving my own home nowadays, even for a night, I decided I would go mad and senile if I didn't get out. I missed little Fang and our walks.

Maybe the perennial nosiness of Littlefold had infected me, but I have to admit to feeling some curiosity about Peter and Jenny. I thought perhaps I might just have lunch with Peter. After all, that had been our practice for many years. But when I telephoned him, it was Jenny who answered. 'Annie? Did you want to speak to Peter? He's not home yet.'

'Oh,' I said lamely. 'Yes. But it's nice to talk to you. How are you, Jenny? Busy with work?'

'Well,' evasive as ever. 'Mmm.'

I continued, 'I thought I could do with a little change. I begin to think I'm getting altogether too Littlefoldian.'

'I know the feeling. Why don't you and Charlie come up and spend a night with us?'

I put this proposal to Charlie who merely said 'No. I've got the grass to cut. You go.'

'But you love Jenny. Don't you want to know what is happening?'

'I like Jenny, yes. But I don't share your avid curiosity about other people's private lives. You go, darling. Have a nice time.'

It was quite obvious when I arrived at the riverside flat that Jenny was playing the part I had so many years ago played while I was with Jack Davidson. It was six o'clock when I got there. Jenny greeted me wearing a blue and white striped apron, and showed me to my room in a matronly fashion. A quick glance through the open door of Peter's bedroom showed it to be well and truly occupied by two. There had been no question of Jenny turning out of the room in which I was to sleep, to accommodate me. I deposited my overnight bag, and very soon Peter appeared and busied himself with drinks, while Jenny served home-made cheese straws. She then disappeared into the kitchen to get on with preparations for dinner.

'I'm very pleased to see you, Annie,' said Peter. 'I left work early this evening.'

'So you're still at the agency?' I asked. 'When are you going to leave, then?'

'I don't really know. The new chap didn't work out. And they offered me a seat on the board if I'd stay on.'

'But Peter...' I said.

'I know. But I won't stay forever. It's only that I feel I ought to support Jenny, just until she gets her business under way.'

For all its elegance, the flat had only one bathroom. In it, I indulged my despicable vice of peering into other people's bathroom cabinets. Charlie always said I ought to

91

be ashamed. So I should be, but I was sure I was not the only transgressor. I've sometimes thought of putting a notice inside ours saying Don't Worry, I Do It Too, although it has to be said that after a certain age, bathroom cupboards become a lot less interesting, owing more to rheumatism, headaches and indigestion than to sex.

My evil prying revealed The Pill, which was obviously working for Jenny, thank goodness, as a half-used box of tampons confirmed.

The conversation at dinner was general. I told Jenny that I missed Fang, and had so much enjoyed going for walks with her mother, the fresh air and exercise had done us both so much good. I was mildly funny at the expense of the Simpsons, and I didn't mention Bill Patterson at all. Peter was rather quiet. Jenny refused to allow either of us to help with the washing up. I formed the impression that far from progressing her new career, she was devoting her entire attention to wifely behaviour. I went to bed feeling fearful but determined to Think Charlie, and mind my own business.

16

It wasn't long after Fang's departure that it was discovered that, as a visitor to Littlefold, he had left an offering behind him. His union with the pug, whose unsuitable name was Prudence, was to be blessed with issue. The owner was not best pleased. The two dogs had only been out of our sight for less than five minutes.

Knowing that the Hon. Miss Featherstone, who had sold Prudence's previous, legitimate litter for large sums, needed the money, I felt extremely guilty at having landed her with a dead loss. I put it to Charlie that the least I could do was to offer to buy one of the little bastards.

Charlie begged me not to, on the grounds that he thought it very likely that Jessie might have to ask us to have Fang again, and that Fang would not like to have what passed for his nose put out of joint. However, resurrecting his executive directorial mind on this occasion, he swept in with what seemed an excellent suggestion. 'You could buy one for Margaret. It would make an excellent Christmas present for her. You could buy two. Give the other to Sally for her brats. It might bite them.'

I thought it would be a good idea if Margaret were to have a puppy. She had so enjoyed Fang's visit. The only way, as I saw it, to accomplish this was to persuade Bill Patterson that it was to be a kind gift from him to his wife. I thought an approach from Charlie would go down better than one from me. He returned from his meeting with a negative report.

'Did he like the idea?' I asked.

'Not a lot. He's already very annoyed, as he puts it, that you coerced his wife into looking after Fang for what he calls days on end.'

'Two days, one night,' I snapped.

'Margaret is a very sick woman, it seems. I get the impression from Bill that she is hardly able to look after herself, never mind a dog. Did you know she was a very sick woman?'

'That's nonsense. She's perfectly sane. She may have been depressed when she tried to drown herself, and I don't blame her, but I assure you she's perfectly sane.'

Charlie had made the one big error of meeting Bill on the man's own territory. At first he had been glad that Margaret was out of sight intending, as he was, to put forward the benevolent idea he had in mind. He had arrived at the evening hour when he and I usually slurp a few pre-prandials, and had been offered a glass of sherry. Having sat for half an hour, trying without success to sell the puppy idea, he asked, 'Will Margaret be joining us?'

'I don't think so,' Bill had said, 'she needs to sleep.'

Charlie now said to me, 'Do you think she was drunk? Bill didn't actually say that, to be fair, but it somehow sounded awfully like it. Anyway, a puppy is out, that's for sure.'

I had no opportunity to ask Margaret whether or not she would like a puppy. I saw less of her now that Fang had gone home.

I tried Sally with no success. She was afraid her sons might go blind if they came in contact with doggie-poo. Charlie thought this was hilarious. 'Goodness, I always thought that was masturbation. That's what I was told, anyway.'

I don't know how Tess Simpson came to hear about Fang's transgression, but that's Littlefold for you. 'Poor

Miss Featherstone,' said Tess, and put in a bid for two puppies.

When I told this to Margaret who was, I am pretty sure, unaware that Bill had turned down a puppy on her behalf, she observed, 'What a good idea. A new smart breed. The Queen has dorgies, why shouldn't the Simpsons have puggineses. And, what's more, puggineses from the Hon. Miss Featherstone's Prudence.'

I had met her in the village shop. She was back to her pre-Fang ways, only venturing out for absolute necessities. At first she didn't notice me, and I observed her casting round in a haphazard fashion, picking up a packet of biscuits, putting it down, and then doing the same with Ryvita, Bakewell tart and chocolate digestive biscuits. At last she said, 'Do you stock brandy? My husband says we've run out.'

A bottle was produced. 'We've got this,' the girl said.

'I expect it will do. I don't know anything about brandy. I suppose it's all right.'

The girl bridled. 'It's VSOP. Very good. It's what Colonel Patterson usually buys.' Margaret accepted and paid for the brandy, turned round and suddenly saw me. Over her shoulder, I saw the girl giving a shrug and a significant look at Mrs Trent who, with her husband, owns the shop. I asked rather sharply for Gentleman's Relish.

The puppies were born in due course. Tess said to me, 'We're paying for ours now, and paying Miss Featherstone to keep them until they are house-trained. I'm afraid I'm a bit fussy about my carpets.'

I knew Tess and Bernard had no children. Neither had I, but somehow I missed out on learning to be fussy about the carpets.

'It's so nice of you to pay for them up-front,' I said. 'I felt awful about letting it happen when she's so fond of Prudence.' And so poor, I didn't add. Charlie called Miss

Featherstone the featherstone in Tess's cap, citing her double value of being aristocratic enough to be desirable, and hard up enough to be pitied. 'I'm sure you'll get a lot of pleasure out of the pups,' I said.

'Yes. The nice thing about dogs is that you meet people, out walking, and get in with them.' I didn't quite know what to say to that, but there was no need. Tess continued, 'I'm so interested in people. I've always been interested in people. My work brought me in touch with interesting people.'

'How interesting,' I said. Because I was grateful to Tess for having assuaged my guilt over Fang's progeny, I continued this tedious conversation, being fool enough to enquire about the job from which she had so profitably retired. I was told, at length, and do not remember one word of it.

The other, and greater guilt I suffered, was at having thrown Jenny and Peter together. I couldn't decide which worried me the more, the prospect of future heartbreak for Jenny, or the prospect of Peter forcing himself to stay in an industry which no longer held any fascination for him. At three o'clock in the morning, Charlie's only contribution to the anxieties I put to him was, 'Go to sleep, you silly old bat, and let nature take its course.'

'Well,' I said, 'at least that it won't. Jenny's on the pill, and she certainly isn't pregnant.'

'Did she tell you so?' yawned Charlie.

'No. I found out.'

'Up to your old tricks? Bathroom cabinets? Really, Annie.'

17

Christmas arrived, approached as usual with cries of shock-horror, what a bore, giving way, equally as usual, to the putting up of holly wreaths on doors and buying of turkeys. Having been the fortunate recipient of my swimming pool-house the year before, this time I found myself not the owner of a puppy, but unexpectedly arraigned as hostess to the Simpsons' puggineses.

Bernard, it seemed, had gone down with flu shortly after the puppies' arrival. No flu jabs? I asked, but not aloud. It was essential, it seemed, that Tess and Bernard should get away to imbibe some sunshine. They booked a Caribbean cruise. I must really be a nicer woman than I give myself credit for, as I refrained from telling Tess that Saga, I had heard, did nice ones.

Tess did ask Miss Featherstone if she would board Flip and Flop, and she certainly would not have been mean about paying for that. But Miss Featherstone was obliged to decline. A well-to-do nephew, it seemed, had invited her to go to his extremely comfortable home for Christmas. As Prudence, apart from her ill-starred sexual proclivities, was a continent and easy-going dog, she was included in the invitation.

'I'm so sorry about poor Mrs Simpson,' Miss Featherstone said to me. 'But I haven't been away for Christmas for twenty years or more. And I do long to go. I believe they have central heating.' Miss Featherstone subsisted with what warmth could be obtained from an inglenook fire in her drawing room, which sucked out more heat than it ever gave in. She also lived, I believe, on a diet of what she grew in the garden and packet fish from the village shop. Prudence was well fed.

'I'll have Flip and Flop,' I said.

'You would, you idiot,' said Charlie. 'Now all we need is for Jessie to get poorly and send Fang here as well and he'll murder the little dears.'

'What, murder his own children?' I said.

'I thought you knew about dogs. He wouldn't even know they were his own children, wouldn't recognise them except as something to be jealous of.'

When Jenny rang me to say, 'I'm coming home for Christmas. I want to see Mummy,' I was pleased with her. I remembered the selfish way in which I had treated my own family during the Jack Davidson days, all to no purpose in the end. I very much hoped the visit would do Margaret good, perhaps bring her out of herself a little, and restore some of the humour I had seen when she and I shared walks with little Fang.

'And Peter?' I asked. 'Is he coming too?'

'Would you be a dear and ask him to stay with you?' I agreed to this. But Peter was evasive and in the end he ducked it, on the grounds that he was taking very little time off over Christmas and it was hardly worth coming away.

Flip and Flop were charming little creatures, though not pretty. Miss Featherstone's house-training had only worked up to a point, or maybe they liked our carpets better than Tess's, the little dears.

At Jenny's request, we ate Christmas dinner in the middle of the day at the Pattersons. I thought it prudent to leave Flip and Flop behind. Apart from anything else, they presented a good excuse for getting away before too long. Charlie had scarcely downed his coffee and

98

thimbleful of cherry brandy before he announced, 'I'm afraid we'll have to go. It's time to let the puppies out.'

'Puppies,' squealed Sally's children as one boy. 'We want to see the puppies.' They refused to take their mother's no for an answer, which entailed a tedious wait while coats and scarves were found and put on, and arguments about who went in which car battled out. At last Sally, Jenny, the two boys, Charlie and I were all at our house. Sally's husband remained behind to keep Bill company, and Margaret went to lie down, having accepted Jenny's offer to do the washing up later. The puppies bounded round the children, licking their faces thoroughly, to Sally's obvious horror. 'We want puppies,' they wailed, having instantly lost interest in the pile of expensive presents they had already demanded and been given.

Jenny was in Littlefold for three days. During that time, no opportunity arose to speak to her alone, which I thought was just as well, as I had no idea what to say. It would be quite unfair to ask her about her mother, and quite impossible to ask her about Peter.

The day after Boxing Day, Margaret came on foot to our house. I felt for her. With Sally and family all over the place, not to mention her own husband, I didn't wonder that she had to get out. She knocked on the door, and I let her in quickly. It was raining, with possible sleet to come. Flip and Flop were entangling my ankles. 'Aren't they endearing?' said Margaret. 'I wish I could have had one of them. It was all our fault that they were born, Annie. I wish I'd had the chance to buy one. I do still have some money of my own.' I was assailed by that stumbling feeling of guilt, as though I had failed, as though I should have stuck it out and fought the Colonel. Still, there was no point in telling her of the opportunity her husband had denied her.

Jenny came to say goodbye. 'I have to go,' she said.

'Back to work?' I enquired.

'Well, I'm thinking about it. But you see, Annie, Peter's working so hard at the moment I really feel it's more important to look after him. I like to have a meal ready when he comes home.'

Her pretty face was so full of love that I hadn't the heart to utter the gloomy warnings of lessons long ago learnt. I waved goodbye and returned to my own thoughts. Charlie was out with the puppies and I was alone in my warm, untidy, cheerful home. And now was good. Charlie had only taken the pups for a short walk along the footpath from our garden but I'd kissed him before he went out. I always do. It may seem silly, since I have been so much loved by my husband for so many years, but I never feel secure. I have never quite got over the fear that what (or whom) I love will be taken from me. Charlie would no more willingly desert me than I would desert him. But I die a little death every time he has to go a motorway journey without me.

For all that I had wiped the slate clean of Jack Davidson well before I married Charlie, I had learnt the hard lesson early that there is no such thing as possessing.

I had recently discovered that Jack was onto his third marriage. The Davidson name often cropped up in the paper. His father, still alive, had, in a roundabout way, inherited a peerage. It was one of those created in the reign of Edward VII, to the chagrin of certain ancient aristocrats at the time, so there was now a title that Jack would inherit. Charlie said, 'You should have stuck it out, darling, you would have been a lady one day!'

I was very glad I hadn't 'stuck it out'. I fell, next time I was alone, to wondering how things would have turned out if I had accepted Jack's invitation to lunch on that long-ago day. Would I have been proof against the pull of that passionate past? I gave myself a vigorous shake, concentrated on now and thanked God I had done no such foolish thing.

The Simpsons had had a wonderful cruise and were deeply grateful to us for looking after Flip and Flop. We were presented with splendid gifts of spectacular uselessness. A satin peignoir for me, two sizes too large... 'I bought it in the ship boutique. You should have seen it, Annie, they had just everything anyone could want.' Charlie's gift was a handsome silk dressing gown two sizes too small. I tried to persuade him to swop.

In the New Year we had a spate of burglaries. It was the opinion of the Littlefold gentry that the council houses were occupied entirely by bad lots whose occupation was milking the system between burgling expeditions and trips to France to buy lorryloads of booze and cigarettes.

Bill Patterson was vocal in this, and acquired an Alsatian dog to guard his property. It was fully grown when he got it, and he announced that its training should be in his hands, women being quite incapable of training dogs. Unfortunately, the only person for whom the animal would do a thing was Margaret. But the dog didn't last long. While out being walked by Bill, who did a great deal of choke-chain jerking and big-stick whacking, it rounded on him, bit a chunk out of his hand and bolted, trailing the leash, straight into the path of a motor-car, thank goodness not mine.

18

That year, I resolved, I really would throw out the old clothes. It was a Wednesday, known in my long-ago agency days as JOW, for Jesus, only Wednesday, as opposed to TGIF.

I had just opened the cupboard in the hall, taken one look and closed it in despair, when I had a visitor.

'Annie,' said a dear and familiar voice. 'I need your help.'

I kissed Peter, and thought, Oh heavens, don't tell me there's been a pill failure.

'May I come in and will you give me a drink?' he asked, adding, 'I have a driver. I'm on business. And I do seriously need your help.'

'Well,' I said, 'if I can. But how did you know I'd be here?'

'I took a chance. I wanted to catch you unawares. If I'd rung to tell you what I wanted, you would have argued.' He then went straight on, 'All my copywriters are illiterate.'

'So were you, when you started.'

'That was different. I had you. But now, even if I enjoyed teaching, which I don't, their combination of arrogance and ignorance endows them with cloth ears. In short, I need some decent copy.'

By now we were sitting comfortably in the kitchen, with a bottle of wine between us. I assumed that Peter had brought with him perhaps one advertisement which I could probably, even after all this time, quite easily lick into shape. I even thought it would be rather fun to get my hands on one page of body copy and turn it into something readable and enticing, perhaps just killing a few banal adjectives and rescuing a couple of verbless sentences. But it wasn't as simple as that.

What rapidly transpired was that Peter wanted me to take on the writing of a whole account. 'What about your driver?' I asked, playing for time. 'Oughtn't he to come in and have some coffee?'

'No,' said Peter. 'I've sent him off to have a look at country graveyards which, for some reason, he happens to enjoy. He'll come back later. Now. About this account. It's a mail-order operation.'

'Oh, Peter. Catalogues? Per-lease,' I wailed.

'No. Not catalogues. They do those themselves. I mean real, proper, full-page selling ads. Magazines, weekend supplements and so on. Not award-winners, I grant you. But nice solid profit, and written for people who can actually read.'

'Old people, you mean. Like me?' I asked.

'Well yes, blurted Peter,' said Peter, softening me up with the old girls-school-story-book verbs we had always enjoyed sharing.

'I really can't, protested Annie,' I countered.

'We pay four hundred pounds a day for top freelance,' said Peter.

I gave this some thought, as I re-filled the glasses. Although Charlie and I always consider we are comfortably off, there is no doubt but that our old house, my lovely pool and our advancing years are expensive items. 'The money sounds lovely, but how on earth could I handle it? Here, I mean.'

'We'd give you a word-processor. The very latest. Internet, E-mail, the lot. All you'd have to do would be to write your copy in the morning and push it through to me before lunch.'

'Peter,' I said, 'I do not know what you are talking about. I've got a typewriter. I write, sometimes, little dreams on it. Even so, I think the ribbon's worn out. I left the business long before all that stuff came in. And if you think I'm going on a computer course, I'm certainly *not*, so there!'

'They aren't that difficult. Everyone uses them. I could send a girl down for a couple of days to show you how to do it. Anyway, I bet Charlie would enjoy it. And he could teach you.'

Charlie, coming in at this point in search of a bottle of Guinness, said, 'Charlie could teach her what?'

'How to use a computer. You'd love it. When Annie's not working on it, you could use it to play games.'

'Such games as I can still manage are perfectly well played without a computer,' said Charlie. 'Anyway, what's this about Annie working?'

Peter explained what we had just been discussing, and I waited for Charlie to come in with sensible objections to my doing anything so foolish as to start in again writing advertisements. His view, once he started to express it, surprised me, although I also found it touching.

'I think it's a very good idea,' he said,' and it would make me feel better, too. I dragged Annie out of the business far too soon, when she still had a lot to offer. She was a saint about it.' I shook my head. 'You were, darling, don't think I don't know. But there is just one thing. In my experience, having freelances making ads in isolation doesn't work. There's no stimulus, no give and take. If you really want Annie to do a good job, you'd do better to take her on, working inside, part-time. Maybe a couple of days a week, but not consecutively. I want her back at night. *J'ai horreur de me coucher seul.*'

104

Charlie was going too fast for me. I said, 'I don't know that I could do it.'

'Of course you could,' he said. 'You never did lose your touch. You're one of the few creative people I ever met who went on doing the nitty-gritty no matter how senior they got.'

'It is what I liked best,' I had to admit.

'We'd pay you as a consultant,' said Peter.

'I like it,' said Charlie. 'We could get the roof repaired.'

'Do you have such a thing as an ordinary typewriter?' I enquired, as I was being swept along by the two of them.

'Not what you'd call an ordinary typewriter. But you know the keyboard. One of the lads can switch it on for you. Or you can write in long-hand if you like. It would be quite amusing to make someone actually read it and type it. Maybe I'd make one of my so-called copywriters do it as an exercise. Oh, Annie, you will do this, please, for my sake.'

'I'll do it while I can do it well and while it's fun. I'm too old to be bored,' I said. On the other hand, what I didn't say was that I was charmed to find I was still seen as worthwhile in a highly competitive and painfully youthful industry. Which brought me back to the point I now had to make to Peter. 'About you, Peter. I appreciate that you are carrying on because you're helping Jenny to get her business project started.' I did not mention the grave doubts I had of her doing any such thing. 'That's good. But didn't I understand that you really wanted to get out of the business?'

'You did, Annie, you did. And I do. And I will, really. But I have to go on earning just for the time being.'

'Peter,' I said, 'you do realise that Jenny is in love with you?'

'Yes,' said Peter, 'I do, and it's giving me a great deal of pleasure. I feel re-manned.'

105

'But what's in it for Jenny?' asked Charlie, the same Charlie who had previously expressed no concern for the girl.

'I hope,' said Peter, 'some enjoyment, some satisfaction. But she won't need me forever. How could she? I'm a tired forty something who made a hash of his first marriage, and she's a stunning twenty-three-year-old. She has the whole world ahead of her. She's beautiful, she's capable, it's all there for her.'

'Do you love her?' I asked.

'Of course I do.'

I had to leave it at that. 'When would you want me to start, given that I agree?' I knew by now that I would be far more sorry if it didn't happen than if it did.

'As soon as possible.'

'If they've banned smoking, the deal's off.'

'We'll give a you a special room to yourself. And I can come in there for a sneaky drag.'

19

I soon found that I needed my swimming pool more than ever. I had forgotten the effect of immobile tension, and I was ridiculously nervous, especially since it seemed it would take at least three of my new colleagues to add up to my age.

Peter, in the powerful position that had come his way *malgré lui*, was endlessly encouraging, humble indeed, in his attitude towards the part-time journeyman copywriter who had once been his boss.

At last I began simply to enjoy what I was doing for a couple of days a week. The youngsters laughed at me, but to my face, not behind my back and not unkindly. I got to know them quite well. Peter, as their creative director, remained somewhat detached from them. I, on the other hand, gave myself the benefit of the simple position I now occupied, and often joined them for lunch. Jenny never came near the place, which was situated in what had, years ago, been known as Fitzrovia. I was taken to Groucho's but I preferred The Three Greyhounds, where the tables wobbled in the way so long ago familiar to me.

They were a likeable bunch, and for all that the ilk of Colonel Patterson would have blown a gasket over some of their ideas, a lot of them didn't seem any barmier to me than my own had been at their age. Indeed, it brought home to me that some of my present attitudes were better kept quiet about in Littlefold. Which brings me to the effect this sporadic but salient detachment from Littlefold had on me.

As the spring went by, it was obvious that the garden would soon suffer from my neglect, I had so much less time and energy for it. Charlie, while he was an inspired grass-cutter, was no weeder or pruner. So we were fortunate to obtain the services of an elderly man called Tom, who had actually worked in this very garden as a boy. After that, he had gone on to bigger things and become a head gardener. Now retired, he was happy to do a bit of jobbing, as he put it, for us. 'Shirt-sleeves to shirt-sleeves,' he said, 'although I never did give up rolling my sleeves back.' I felt his position was very much like my own, and we took to each other right away.

I actually began to see rather more of Margaret Patterson than I had for some time. Where, before, I had been a little hesitant except during the Fang-walking phase, I now called on her occasionally. She would ask if I had seen Jenny, and I would reply rather vaguely, 'I'm always at work when I'm in town, and I don't stay over.'

'No,' she said, 'and of course Jenny's very busy too, isn't she, with her catering project.' I really was quite unsure of what, if anything, Jenny had lately told her mother.

My London days were Monday and Thursday. I went up by train. Charlie took me to the station, and picked me up on my return. 'But darling,' I said, 'won't this be a bore for you? I mean, having to turn out every evening to meet me?'

'I like to do it,' he said, 'I do owe you something, you know. In any case, coming to meet you means I can't have a drink until I've got you safe at home. And that is good for me.'

'Are you bored when I'm not here?' I asked.

'Don't kid yourself. I've got my interests.'

'Tess Simpson's painting group?'

'No. Painting's not my thing. But I do see her occasionally. We both call on Miss Featherstone.'

Charlie, it seemed, had taken to mowing Miss Featherstone's grass. I thought this was lovely of him, so merely said, 'Have a care. Knowing you, you'll trash her herb garden while you're at it.'

That Miss Featherstone was quite the fashion in Littlefold was lost on him. It transpired that she had asked him if I would like some herbs. As he didn't know fennel from feverfew, I was invited to come over and choose what I would like to have.

I found Miss Featherstone not only highly entertaining but also extremely informative. 'Now, do pop over whenever you need anything. Charlie tells me you are a most excellent cook.'

'So-so,' I said, 'I like feeding people.'

'He also tells me you are doing your proper job again. I think that is wonderful. I wish I had been trained to do something lucrative.'

'I wasn't really trained at all,' I said, 'I just got lucky.'

'Now Mrs Simpson, she was trained like billy-ho, I believe. She's quite a nice creature in her way. Terrific snob. That appalling Patterson is very keen on her.'

'You don't mean?' I said.

'No, not that. Not an *affaire*.' Her pronunciation told of some-time finishing school in France. 'She is far too Littlefoldised for that. And he, of course, is faithful to his poor mad wife.'

'Margaret Patterson is not mad,' I said.

'She must be, to have married that fearful little upstart.'

'Have you met her mother?' I asked.

'Yes. You probably didn't notice, but I was at that party they gave a couple of summers ago. I went for the champagne. I love champagne. Alas, it turned out to be rather less than champagne. I didn't fall in love with Mrs

109

Watershed or whatever her name might be, but she did at least know that what we were drinking was rubbish. Actually, I didn't really mind her. She is at least of my generation.'

I was astounded. 'You can't possibly be as old as Mrs Wallingford.'

'I'm eighty-four,' said Miss Featherstone.

'I would have put you at about seventy,' I said.

'Nice of you to say so.'

'It's quite true.'

Miss Featherstone was snipping off herbs as she spoke. 'As I said, better come here for them than try to grow these yourself. It will give me pleasure. Yes. Well. I suppose it's because I never married. Marriage can be a very ageing experience for a woman. Incidentally, I beg your pardon. Margaret Patterson is a friend of yours? I shouldn't have made that remark, picked up, as it was, simply from gossip.'

Prudence came waddling up, and changed the subject. 'Flip and Flop seem to be a great success with the Simpsons,' I said, thanked Miss Featherstone for the herbs, and went home.

Peter had telephoned in my absence. 'I said you'd call him back,' said Charlie. What Peter wanted was to ask if I would give him an extra day the following week. I said no.

Charlie, hearing this, waited until I had rung off and then said, 'Do if you'd like to.'

'I don't like,' I said, 'unless you want to get rid of me.'

'No. But I want you to do whatever you think best.' I blessed him for not saying 'whatever you want to do.'

I stuck to my two days and thoroughly enjoyed them. The money was good, and useful, but we really didn't need more. Charlie, in his capacity of what he cheerfully called 'the little woman at home', had begun to enlarge our social circle. Quite soon we were invited to dinner with Miss Featherstone. I was highly amused that Bill Patterson and the Simpsons had not been invited.

It was a delightful experience. Charlie and I had, between us, quite a few family bits and pieces, and, during our heyday years, we had also acquired more, but never in my life had I seen such a dinner table as hers, though the table itself was as wobbly as the tables at The Three Greyhounds. 'Its legs are past their best, like mine,' said Miss Featherstone.

Perhaps if Miss Featherstone had married and had children, the 200-year-old wine glasses would not have survived. The silver was slender with aeons of butler-polishing.

'Do come,' she had said. 'Just the two of you, and my nephew and his wife.'

The food! Miss Featherstone had made of one chicken from the village shop a delicacy beyond compare. With her own herbs and a sauce she had learnt to make at Clermont Ferrand, it was preceded by a superb consommé (the chicken bones, no doubt) and succeeded by ice cream. 'Bought, I'm afraid. I haven't the means of making it. No freezer. The plums are mine, though.' They were those delicious little wild plums. Then came a savoury, mushrooms on toast. 'I was lucky they began so early this year. They are puffballs, actually.' I would have blenched had I not by now gained complete faith in Miss Featherstone's knowledge of all things that grew.

I found myself quite chatty. When the nephew's wife spoke of her young, with affectionate disparagement, 'I mean, a frock that looks like granny's liberty silk, worn with bovver boots,' I was able to counter with, 'They're not called bovver boots any more. I know it looks awful at first but I've got used to it with my young people.'

'Your grandchildren?' the wife asked.

111

'No, my colleagues,' I replied with some satisfaction.

I saw Margaret a couple of days later, and learnt that Bill had been very upset at not being invited to Miss Featherstone's dinner. 'But Margaret,' I said, 'surely he couldn't be. Everyone knows you hardly ever go out.'

'So it seems.'

'So obviously she wouldn't ask Bill without you.'

'Everyone else does.'

'But Miss Featherstone's old-fashioned.'

'Not all that more old-fashioned than the rest of Littlefold. Poor Bill, I'm a burden to him.'

'Has he said so?'

'Not in so many words. But he does tell me he worries about me; about the state of my mind. I worry about it myself. You know, Annie, sometimes I don't quite know what I'm doing.'

'In what way?' I asked.

'Oh, I lose things, put things in funny places. I find things I don't remember anything about. Sometimes I think I'm going mad. Sometimes I even wish I was dead.'

Only in the most complete privacy had Charlie and I talked to each other about the episode in our swimming pool. Even Charlie, who is so against exaggeration that I sometimes suspect he would describe a broken back as a slight touch of fibrositis, had to agree with me that Margaret had not simply fainted and fallen in.

It did cross my mind that I ought to have a word with Jenny. I thought it might be helpful to Margaret to be taken more into her daughter's confidence, in short, to be made to feel useful. But somehow, I didn't get the opportunity, and I certainly wouldn't have consulted Sally.

I was absolutely determined that I would not extend my working commitment to more than two days a week. As a result, those two days were intensely busy. Peter, although always courteous and complimentary, necessarily became more and more remote. Occasionally I would ask, 'How's Jenny?', and be told she was fine.

About this time, Mrs Wallingford came for a short visit. This time, the Pattersons did not give a party. To my surprise, she only stayed a couple of days, and then took Margaret home with her. I learnt this from Tess Simpson. She said to me, without malice but with conviction, 'I'm so glad Margaret has gone to stay with her mother for a while. Poor Bill needs a break.'

'Does he?' was all I could muster in reply.

'Oh dear me, yes. He cares for her with such devotion. It can't be easy for him. He's wonderful, though. But it seems she is reaching a point where she can't be left on her own. She can't really do a thing.'

This comment tied in with the pathetic outburst I had recently heard from Margaret. I was not only sad but also puzzled. Was this the same woman, the Margaret little Fang had so much liked, whose company I had so much enjoyed on our walks? 'How do you mean, she can't do a thing?' I asked.

'It isn't for me to say any more, when I know how much of a friend you have been to her, Annie. You're very loyal.' She made loyalty sound like some kind of a weakness on my part.

I merely said, 'Well, she's a very nice woman and I always enjoy her company.'

Tess had the last word. 'You're very kind. But then, you're not around much these days, are you, so perhaps you haven't noticed how weary Bill sometimes looks. It's very sad.'

20

Although my young colleagues were rendered aghast at the prospect of a constructed sentence and dedicated to making art-directed but totally incomprehensible television commercials, they really were an endearing bunch.

I decided against any attempt to introduce them to Littlefold, even though I had my lovely swimming pool to offer. Anyway, apart from the ghastly prospect of bringing them face to face with Bill Patterson or Tess Simpson, they all took, when their holiday times came round, vacations in such places as Las Vegas, Hong Kong, Buenos Aires and Phuket. They were so much *not* Littlefold that I sometimes felt as though I was conducting a secret love affair.

One of the more conscientious ones did a stint in the Balkans and returned, I am thankful to say, alive. This one was a young woman called Florence. She let on that her parents were educated, 'like you,' as she put it. 'Me?' I stuttered. 'Coo.'

Florence was what used to be described in my youth as A Nice Girl. This meant, as it always has meant, that she had no sex appeal at all. She also had the misfortune to be in love with Peter Baker. For this wistful reason, she had got to know Jenny. I knew Jenny never came to the office. But Florence had used the old trick of having some work so urgent that she had to take it round to the boss's home, which is how she came to realise that Peter had a live-in girlfriend, and an extremely attractive one at that.

The occasions on which I lunched with two or three of the young ones were great fun. They knew I never stayed long. Apart from the fact that my desk really was piled up with work, I had enough sense to make myself scarce, I hoped before I bored them. But then came the day when Florence invited me to lunch. It was, as I expected, at a vegetarian restaurant, all nuts and freshly squeezed fruit juices. I didn't mind the sobriety, I was usually cautious at lunch-time. But when poor Florence's confidences began, I started to wish I had at least a carafe of something to make me feel less awkward.

Peter, it seemed, was the most wonderful creative director in the world. I came in for my share of flattery. 'I know you trained him, Annie, he thinks the world of you, and so do I. I like to think my copy is rather like yours.' Florence's position in the agency was that of copywriter on such products as walk-in-baths, stair lifts and such things as prevent the elderly from toppling over. Her prose was grammatical, true, but quite monumentally dull. Fortunately, the art directors and typographers conspired to see it was printed in such a way that no one, even with the brightest eyes in the world, could possibly read it.

While I tried not to look at my watch, we progressed to Jenny, a lovely girl but not quite right for Peter. 'I know her very well,' I said hastily, 'in fact I've known her since she was a schoolgirl. Her parents are friends of ours, neighbours.'

I could see Florence grinding to change gears. 'Oh well, she is a sweet person, of course. It's just that she's so young. It worries me.'

It worried me, too. But, worry or not about Jenny, I could hardly advise Florence to wait in the wings for disaster in that quarter. Even though I feared it must come, it was unlikely to open the door for Florence. I merely said, 'Peter was married, years ago. I don't think he is likely ever to marry again.' Florence folded her lips and looked at me with hatred disguised as charity. Lunch concluded.

I went for a brisk walk after this, pausing only to buy myself a large cup of very strong coffee, and then got back to finish my work. I telephoned Charlie and asked if it would be convenient for him to meet me earlier than usual. I scribbled as fast as I could. I wanted to get home to Charlie.

In the train I couldn't help thinking how unfair it was that however ill-chosen Jenny's course of love might be, she had the enormous advantage of dark blue eyes, fabulous eyelashes and a sort of appeal that was all the more compelling because she was not particularly conscious of it.

Tom was at work in the garden when we got home. I had told him to come at whatever hours he chose. He had become rather arthritic and found himself considerably more mobile after a couple of lunch-time beers in the pub. 'Is beer good for arthritis?' I asked him, to be told, 'It is for mine.'

Whatever his elected medicine, Tom's effect on the garden was stupendous. The roses bloomed and bloomed, with never a greenfly to be seen. 'I breathe on them and puff my pipe on them,' he said. I was glad that my new earning power went a little way towards providing Tom with a few of the pleasures of old age which had, in the bad old days, been taken for granted.

I had a swim, while Charlie cooled a bottle of wine. What luxury, I thought, at my time of life, to come home from work and be asked the usually wifely question, 'Had a good day at the office, darling?'

I sipped my glass of wine. 'I had freshly squeezed cantaloupe juice at lunch,' I said.

116

'Good Lord, why?' asked Charlie.

'I had lunch with our Florence. She's a vegetarian. She doesn't drink and she doesn't smoke.'

'Well, at least, does she do the other?'

'Poor girl, it doesn't look like it. She's in love with Peter.'

'Oh dear. Another Jenny?'

'Not in the least like Jenny. She has white eyelashes.'

'Perhaps you could teach her how to dye them.'

I didn't really think that would help. I said as much, and added, 'There's a word-processor on my desk.'

On my next office day, Peter came into my room to tell me that if I really hated the thing and didn't want to learn it, they would get me an easy electric typewriter instead. For the first time in quite a while, he sat down and stayed for half an hour.

While he was there, Florence appeared. I had a pretty good idea that she had seen him making his way in my direction. 'Oh Annie,' she said, 'I wonder if you would be kind enough to cast your eye over this copy for me? Oh Peter, I didn't know you were here. Please, don't let me interrupt.'

'That's all right,' said Peter. 'We were just talking word processors. Annie's a bit daunted. Perhaps you'd give her some help; a lesson or two.'

'I'm not very clever at that sort of thing.' Florence, who knew all there was to know about word-processors, faxes, internet, e-mail from wwws to the last dot, fluttered her useless eyelashes.

As soon as Peter left the room, she forgot all about her alleged reason for coming, and departed, copy in hand. I felt sorry for her but I couldn't really worry too much about her.

Apart from anything else, things were happening in Littlefold which engaged much more of my concern.

117

21

Margaret Patterson, it seemed, had decided to stay on a little longer with her mother.

I had a note from her. *Dear Annie, I will be away for a few days more than I had planned. My mother isn't very well. I will feel happier if I stay here while I am of use to her.* This rather formal little communication ended, touchingly, with *Your loving friend, Margaret.*

All this time, I had been enjoying my new-found capacity in my old trade, not without thinking about Jenny but totally without being in touch with her. Now, I thought I would go and pay a call on Margaret, after which I could legitimately see Jenny with news of her mother.

As Margaret's letter gave no address or telephone number, merely Eastbourne and the date, I was obliged to approach Bill. I had developed such a dislike for Bill Patterson that I was gushingly polite to him. 'Bill,' I said, having forced myself to go to the house. 'I'm so sorry to hear that your mother-in-law is ill.'

'Not very,' he replied. 'Liver, mostly, I suspect. I fear she has brought it on herself.'

'Well,' I said, 'it's nice for her to have Margaret there for a while.'

'Yes, maybe. It's rather sad, but I'm afraid a lot of my wife's problems stem from that source.'

'If you please?' I asked, as graciously as I could, 'may I have Mrs Wallingford's telephone number?'

'If you really must,' said Bill. But I got it out of him.

I punched out the numbers and was answered by Mrs Wallingford herself. 'This is Annie Finlay,' I said.

'Oh.' The unwelcoming voice did not surprise me, so I continued as sturdily as I had with Bill Patterson. 'I believe Margaret is staying with you at the moment. Isn't that nice?' How fatuous, I wondered, could one sound.

'Yes. Do you wish to speak to her?' I said that yes, I would like to do that.

In reply to my opening 'How are you?' Margaret said, 'Very well, thank you.' She sounded a little detached, so I continued with, 'And how is your mother?'

'Not terribly well.'

I came to the point. 'I would like to see you. Would you like to see me?'

'That would be very nice.'

'Shall we fix a day? I could easily drive over and perhaps you would both like to come out to lunch with me.'

'That's sweet of you, but I think it would be better if you let me give you some lunch here. My mother's appetite is tiny and she always says she can't cope with the huge helpings they give in restaurants.'

I agreed to this and set off for Eastbourne the following Tuesday. Mrs Wallingford, when first I had met her, had given the impression of living in poky circumstances, so I was unprepared for her apartment. She had referred to a balcony. This balcony, overlooking the sea, was more like a conservatory, filled with well-tended flowering shrubs. There was even a plumbago. Margaret hung my coat in a vast closet in the hall, from where I could see into the bedrooms, three of them, the largest of them presumably Mrs Wallingford's and every one quite clearly the sort that has its own bathroom. The sitting room could only be described as a drawing room, a door opening out of it into the dining room. No wobbly tables pulled up to the armchairs for Mrs Wallingford. It wouldn't have surprised me if lunch had been served by a maid in black with a white apron. However, Margaret, having seated me comfortably, disappeared.

'My housekeeper's on holiday this week,' said Mrs Wallingford, thus giving rise to my own uncharitable thought that maybe she had retained Margaret rather more for that reason than for the not-very-well explanation.

'I let her do a bit of cooking, it's therapy for her. She's pathetically lacking in self-confidence,' murmured Mrs Wallingford, drinking a gin and tonic which Margaret had given her before going out to the kitchen. I sipped carefully at the very small glass of excellent sherry which was all I had accepted on account of the car.

Margaret served us with a cheese soufflé, excellently *à pointe*, and a perfect salad. 'No salad for me,' said Mrs Wallingford, 'you know I can't digest it.'

'Yes, mother, I do know. Look, I've done you some runner beans.'

'Same thing,' said Mrs Wallingford, taking one spoonful of the soufflé, for which I was thankful, as I took the lion's share, thinking hard luck if she changes her mind. I could see what a good wine was being served, but I also went easy on that, breathalyser in mind, which made me all the hungrier.

An Apple Betty followed. 'Not crême brulée?' said Mrs Wallingford. 'You know crême brulée is the only pudding I like.'

'And you also know you can't have two eggy dishes in the same meal,' said Margaret with spirit.

Mrs Wallingford laughed. 'I can have as many eggy dishes as I like. All this nonsense about cholesterol.'

'I'll go and make the coffee,' said Margaret.

Mrs Wallingford led the way back into the drawing room, having added, 'And for heaven's sake make it strong enough. I can't stand dishwater.' She sat in a not-too-low chair and crossed one thin leg over the other. I was pretty sure she wasn't very comfortable but I couldn't help but admire the vanity of it. 'Now, Mrs Finlay,' she began.

'Annie, please,' I demurred.

'Very well, then, Annie, since I am your senior by a good many years.' This made it clear that she was to remain Mrs Wallingford to me. She then went straight on with what she wanted to say while Margaret was out of the room. 'You probably think I'm a very unpleasant old woman. I am. I never was a kindly creature but, now that I am old, I can no longer be bothered to care what anyone thinks of me. I mean to live my remaining years as I wish, and don't think my saying "remaining years" is in any way pathetic. I do not intend that foolish girl to inherit for a very long time. If I die, that appalling husband of hers will have her in the loony bin, toute suite, and grab the lot. For that reason, I keep my own counsel as to my means.' I felt pretty sure that Mrs Wallingford had been, and probably still was, a shrewd investor. She continued, 'There would have been no problem if we had had a son to inherit but there it is! Poor Margaret. I know all mothers are supposed to think their sons-in-law are not good enough for their daughters, but when Margaret married Patterson I was, quite simply, glad to marry her off at all. He has always disliked me and I have always disliked him.'

At this point, Margaret appeared with the coffee, and I hoped she had not overheard. She gave no sign of having done so. Mrs Wallingford drank her coffee and pronounced it 'passable'.

'I need to rest now. I find visitors quite exhausting,' she announced. I, as the visitor, was not in the least exhausted. I had been riveted, the whole time. However, I took the point, and was escorted by Margaret to my car. 'It was so good of you to come,' she said. I told her I had very much wanted to come, and she added, 'I am very fond of you, and so is my Jenny. I don't know what you made of my mother.'

'I found her most interesting, and I have thoroughly enjoyed seeing her again.' This was perfectly true, as I had found Mrs Wallingford's conversation quite fascinating.

Margaret and I parted affectionately, with an assurance on my part that I would make a point of seeing Jenny as soon as possible.

22

Then one day, Peter pushed his way through the pulsating youngsters, found me tapping away on my electronic typewriter, and invited me to have lunch with him. 'I'm so busy, Peter,' I protested.

'I do desperately need to talk to you. It's about Jenny, really.'

I began to wonder how much I really knew about Jenny. I was fond of her, for sure. But I had rather (perhaps arrogantly) equated her ill-promising love affair with my own of all those years ago, from which I had so completely recovered. It was very quiet in my little office. 'Why not let us talk here?' I said.

The door was thrown open, and one of the account handlers burst in. Knocking on doors before entering went out with advertisements that told you what the product was. Peter was sitting in the only chair other than mine. Carl parked his plump buttock on the corner of my desk. I rescued my paper-cup of coffee just in time to save a pile of freshly typed copy.

'Annie,' said Carl in a voice of enthusiasm, 'you'll love this. It's a whole better way for your mail order. Internet. We're going internet.'

'Tell me about it, Carl dear,' I said, 'some other time.' I had no intention of getting into an explanation that readers of these particular ads were unlikely to use internet, so I merely added, 'Right now, Peter wants to talk to me.' This had no effect, so, obliged to alter my refusal to go out, I said firmly, 'And we are just going out to lunch. See me later.'

'Good,' said Peter. 'Come along.'

I was amazed that there was one place in the vicinity that didn't know anything about the profitability of feeding advertising moguls. They didn't know who Peter was. 'Have you booked a table?' he was asked, more in bravado than in hope. They then just managed to fit us in, in the agreeable silence of some ten empty placements.

'I am very fond of Jenny,' said Peter, not eating his gnocchi.

'So am I,' I said, 'and as you know, her mother is a good friend of mine. I've just been to see her. She is staying with *her* mother. And naturally I imagine she would like to hear some news of her daughter. Can you tell me anything about her catering project?' I spoke dully and hurriedly because I was anxious.

'Yes, no, well, Annie, I'm trying to get her to grow out of me.'

'You'll be telling me next that you're not good enough for her.'

'Something like that.'

'That one was used when I was a girl,' I said. 'You mean you don't love her as she loves you.'

'Maybe I don't. In a funny way, I think I love her more than she loves me. I'll certainly miss her, but it's her I'm thinking of. It's sad. There will never be anyone else like her.'

'A good excuse with other women later,' I said tartly.

'It's true. I've never been loved the way Jenny loves me. I said to her, what about when I do leave the advertising business, and I'm just an ageing bloke trying to write a book that will never be published?'

'I think you'll find it would make no difference to her.'

'So she says. But she doesn't know what she's talking

about. She's such a simple darling, she doesn't realise that we're living in the lap of phony luxury.'

'So are we. Well, up to a point. But I must tell you that what you are paying me is setting up the Finlay homestead rather promisingly.' This was true. It was also true that I was aware that the day Peter should quit his directorship would see the end of my renaissance. But Peter was speaking again, so I gave him my attention.

He drew in breath. 'I'm going to break it off, Annie. It's only fair to do it while she's still young and still so pretty.'

'You mean so pretty she'll easily attract another lover. You men!' I snarled. And yet, for all I had forever loathed the masculine attitude towards a woman's need for a man in her life, however much I told myself that times had changed since my day, I could point to very few young women who voluntarily opted for celibacy. Unmarried maternity, yes. Unmarried cohabiting, yes. Postponement of lasting commitment, often until too late, yes. But no one of her own to sleep with for a girl, no. 'I have to say that I don't care for your opinion,' I said. 'But on the other hand, I suppose she'll get over it.'

'I very much hope so. I'll do it as carefully as I can. It's not easy, but it serves me right. I should never have let it happen.'

'Is it really impossible, Peter?' I asked.

'What do you think? I'm twenty years older than she is. I never intend to get married again. I don't want children. I'm working class, she's upper class.'

'Oh, class,' I scoffed. 'Bollocks, Peter. Now really, that's one thing that *has* changed. However, if you really feel it's not on, better do it and get it over with. I'd rather she didn't end up like her unfortunate mother.' I was making little headway with my duck salad, and Peter's gnocchi now looked like greasy pebbles. The proprietor, who was

125

also his own chef and waiter, came anxiously to the table. 'You have not enjoyed your food?' he said, clearly upset.

'It's delicious,' I said, 'but unfortunately we neither of us are very well. It must be something we ate yesterday, elsewhere.'

'I bring you soup. Minestrone. Multo digestible.'

I dreaded the arrival of soup, also to be uneaten. 'We'll come again and do justice to your food. Just now, my son and I would like coffee and grappa.' He beamed at my lie, now able to place me where I should respectably belong. 'I suppose heartbreak at twenty-three is better than despair later,' I said. 'You don't know, of course, that Margaret Patterson tried to drown herself in our swimming pool.'

'No, I didn't know that. Jenny doesn't talk much about her family, except that her sister has two little boys. I know her mother is said to be delicate. That's all I know, except for what little I've seen when I've been visiting you. The old man's a prick, that's for sure. Very different from your own lovely Charlie.'

'Very different indeed. Talking of which, Peter, I really want to get back to work and then get home. It's all very well for me, I've been drinking a carafe of wine and grappa as well, oh dear, how bossy of me, and Charlie comes to the station and doesn't even have a beer until he's got me safely home.'

On the way home from the station, I said abruptly to Charlie, 'Peter is going to ditch Jenny.'

'Poor Jenny,' said Charlie, striving unsuccessfully to control his irritation at being unable to overtake a vast vehicle laden with bales of straw that looked like giant toilet rolls. 'Bugger these things. Still, she'll get over it. She's young, and she's very pretty.'

'You too!' My foodless lunchtime had left me in a sour mood. 'You think it's as easy as that?'

'Well, you did it. And you got lovely me.'

'Don't crow. You're too sober by half. Let's get home so you can imbibe a little and get less complacent.'

Charlie had forgotten to disinter anything from the freezer for supper. I wasn't cross. 'Shall we go out?' he asked guiltily.

'No,' I said. 'There's bacon in the fridge, and eggs. I'll make something, no bother.' Tom's tomatoes were ripe. We had a very good supper indeed made by me, and I was proud of it. I tried not to think about what sort of an evening Jenny was having.

23

Jenny came back to Littlefold. I now had the terrible experience of witnessing her broken heart. When my own heart had been broken, I had at least had the makings of a career to fill my days and to shore up my pride. It was obvious, and really had been all along, that Jenny had totally eschewed the idea of professional catering.

The mores of my day had decreed that I must be secretive with my family. Strangely enough, even in this day and age, the same applied to Jenny. Her sister was steeped in being a married lady with children. Her father was a cold, self-centred man whose own conceit was dependent upon condemning others. As to her mother, poor Margaret had her own troubles.

I had seen for myself that Jenny was looking dreadful, so I was hardly surprised when Charlie said to me, 'Your poor little friend is not in good shape.' He had seen her on his way home from mowing Miss Featherstone's grass.

'Did you speak to her?' I asked.

'Only slightly. I just said, 'Nice to see you, Jenny.' She said something I could hardly hear, and turned away. I don't wonder, poor child. She's become as plain as a pikestaff, these days.'

'What,' I asked, 'is a pikestaff?'

'I don't know,' said Charlie testily. 'I only know she's utterly miserable and she's lost her looks.'

When I had been deserted, the first thing that happened to me was that I got very thin. I had been sick while I was pregnant, and had nearly bled to death after the abortion. Furthermore, I had driven myself at a frantic pace in my job. Working was the only bearable part of my day and I would go on for hour after hour. I had no appetite and made no attempt to gain one. I realise now that I had at the time a rather pathetic hope that I would become ill unto death, and that Jack would appear heartbroken at my bedside and all would be well.

With Jenny, I found that her tragedy was manifesting itself in a different way. Now living at home, she had nothing to do. She was obviously nibbling. Her face was puffy, which diminished the beauty of her dark blue eyes. The first time I saw her I hardly recognised her. She was plodding along the village street. I was behind her. She had the rounded shoulders of fat misery. It wasn't until I overtook her and looked back that I realised this really was my friend Jenny. I said hallo and she answered hallo in a voice of total lethargy.

I wished I could comfort her. But it would hardly have helped if I had taken it upon myself to say, 'You'll get over it, I did.' For one thing, I was by no means certain that Jenny would get over it.

In my own case, I had been ruthlessly and insultingly rejected. It was perfectly clear that there was not, and never would be, any place for me in Jack's Orthodox and profoundly enclosed Jewish family.

Peter was a very different proposition from Jack Davidson. Jack was as mother-spoiled as only a boy from a rich Jewish family can be, not so much born with a silver spoon as born with the full canteen. My pregnancy was almost certainly the first grown-up problem he had ever had to face, except that he refused to face it.

Peter, on the other hand, had come up the hard way. From very humble, scarcely educated beginnings, he had fallen into my bossy aegis, which he had survived to become the mature leader he now was. And although he had no intention of marrying again, he was far from being as irresponsible or ruthless as that implied. I could imagine only too well the gentle kindness with which he would have tried to explain to Jenny that it was all over.

At work, I avoided Peter. Well, I think Peter avoided me. I wasn't exactly angry with him, and I can't really say that I wished the whole thing had never happened; experience, after all, must take place. But the sight of Jenny's utter wretchedness was heartbreaking to me.

One of the most depressing aspects of the whole affair was that Jenny, poor rejected Jenny was spending day in, day out, in the dismal confines of the parental home. We had a lot of rain as autumn came on, pattering on the fallen leaves with persistent fretfulness.

It would have been nice if Sally had emerged as a supportive big sister. But Sally was far too busy with her matronly duties to concern herself with silly Jenny who seemed, Sally told me on one occasion when we had all convened for Patterson Sunday lunch, to have made a fool of herself with 'that friend of yours in London, Peter Something.'

Margaret had returned from her mother's, so I went to visit her. Bill opened the door to me and led me into the sitting room, where he invited me to sit down. For a brief moment, I let myself think he was about to express some fatherly concern about his younger daughter's plight. I was seated in a large, low armchair. Bill took an upright desk chair from which he looked down at me. 'I won't beat about the bush,' he said, 'I'm a plain man, so I'll come straight to the point. I'm worried about Jenny.'

'So are we,' I said hopefully.

'So you agree with me that she's looking terrible. I know all women lose their looks eventually, but not at her age, surely.'

'I think she's very unhappy,' I ventured.

'What on earth has she got to be unhappy about? I let her go to London to do whatever she chose to do there, but apparently that didn't suit her. And now she's home, doing absolutely nothing, eating her head off. I tried to get the job at the estate agent's back for her but my friend there doesn't want her, after the way she walked out. The trouble with the young these days is that they think of nobody but themselves.'

'Weren't we all a bit like that?' I asked.

'I wasn't.' Bill was quite definite on that score. 'I was already an officer by the time I was her age. I had a sense of duty.' I agreed hastily, hoping we might get somewhere. We did. 'And of course her mother's absolutely no help to me,' Bill continued. 'Since she's come back from *her* mother's I can only say she might just as well have stayed away. She's never out of her room. What she does there I tremble to think.'

I was not going down that road, so I just did my best to appear helpful. 'Well,' I said, 'this is all a worry for you, I do see. As you know, my job takes me to town twice a week but I've plenty of time free otherwise. I'll try and get Jenny to come over and swim again. That way, at least she might begin to get more fit.'

I hoped the concept of getting fit might have pleased the old soldier, for he paused to thank me, briefly. He then went on, 'I'm a troubled man, you know. I have a lot of duties in the parish, and it's very difficult when one is under perpetual strain at home. The magazine expects my piece every month.' Indeed! A tedious little piece under the byline AN OLD SOLDIER, regularly appeared.

I gave up hope of seeing Margaret that day, but later on I got hold of Jenny and suggested she come over to our house for a swim. She agreed in a manner I would

131

have interpreted as rude if I hadn't been so aware of the wretchedness of the speaker.

One day, Charlie appeared while Jenny and I were in the pool. My husband may be getting on a bit but he is still all man. But any hope that his masculine presence might perk Jenny up was forlorn. She had reverted to her sister Sally's unbecoming swimsuit, her legs and armpits could clearly do with a good waxing job, and she let her uncared-for hair drag in the water.

I tried to get Dick and Desmond to persuade her to go back to the Casuarina Tree but, unfortunately, a new girl had had to be taken on in her place. 'We don't like her half as much as Jenny. But there was no alternative, we had to have someone.'

The only thing I could think of that was in any way positive was to try and do something about Jenny's appearance. Obviously feeling ugly, she seemed to be going out of her way to dress ugly, frequently in a shapeless T-shirt of that peculiarly depressing shade of bottle green that makes you wonder how anyone could have bought it in the first place. The shape, I presumed, was due to having been washed a lot but not, alas, recently.

If I had only been able to get her back to the Casuarina Tree, I believed I might have been able to persuade her to smarten herself up a bit, for very pride. She had always been 'pretty Jenny' to the elderly customers who liked her so much.

24

I felt like a heron with two different ponds to swoop upon. One, the advertising agency in London, the other, Littlefold. In London, my new young friends in the creative department were getting desperate about their approaching geriatry. Those nearing thirty were looking anxiously at the teenagers coming in. 'What *is* Peter about?' they asked me. 'Peter was a teenager when I hired him,' I replied placatingly.

Peter himself was very gloomy company at this time. He had made the mistake of being kind to the besotted Florence. It hadn't taken Florence, whose antennae were always waving in his direction, long to find that Jenny was out of the scene.

In pursuit of her heart's desire, Florence now set about bucking up her ideas. She lowered her neckline and raised her copy, or so she hoped. The result was like watching an aardvark getting sprauncy. Peter, in professional despair, showed me one of her offerings, which I was obliged to confiscate and rewrite. He really should have got rid of her. With Florence after him, and doggedly so, I rather meanly said to him, 'Oh well then, out of the frying pan into the wok.'

Then came the evening when I arrived home from work to learn from Charlie the disturbing news that dear Miss Featherstone was not at all well. He had Prudence, wearing a mournful expression on her puggy face, in the car. 'I had a job to get her to come with me, she's not used to men.' Prudence crept into my lap. Charlie went on, 'I said we'd keep her for the night.'

'What is the matter with Miss Featherstone?' I asked.

'She says it's just a chill, and she wouldn't hear of having the doctor. So I made her go to bed and gave her some tea and an aspirin. I promised we'd take Prudence back to her tomorrow.'

We managed to cheer Prudence up with a share of our own dinner, fillet steak that night, which she thought well of. Later on, she stayed close to me and indicated her intention of following me upstairs at bedtime. At this, Charlie asserted his rights as Master Of The House. 'No, Prudence,' he said.

Prudence was persuaded to sleep on a cushion in the kitchen, with a chocolate digestive biscuit for consolation. In the morning, I took her for a walk and then back to Miss Featherstone's house. Miss Featherstone was up and about and declared herself perfectly well, but it was obvious that she was not. As it was not one of my working days, I had enough free time to take a bossy stance with Miss Featherstone, although this was not an easy thing to do.

Luckily, I had not been long at Miss Featherstone's when Charlie appeared, just as I was getting nowhere with her. She and I were in the kitchen, and I had just managed to catch a Sèvres plate as it slipped out of her shaking fingers. Charlie put his arm round her, and led her into the sitting room. The house was cold. He lit the fire, which smoked. He was holding her hands, a liberty Miss Featherstone seemed to enjoy.

Then Tess Simpson arrived. 'I heard you were poorly, so I came at once,' she cried.

'I don't know where you heard that. I am perfectly all right. I am just having a chat with Mr Finlay.'

'What can I do for you? How can I help you?' asked

134

Tess, sounding remarkably like those females who answer the telephone when your washing machine has gone wrong and it's going to cost you £40 for a call-out charge.

'I need no help, thank you, I have everything I require. So, very kind of you as it was to come, there is no need for you to stay. You are such a busy lady.' Having got rid of Tess in short order, she then said to me, 'I can't stand that woman when I am well, and just now, I feel very ill.'

Between us, Charlie and I dragged her up to her bedroom. She made no objection to Charlie's presence, even though I am fairly certain she had never before been undressed by a man. I managed to find a hot water bottle, one which I imagined had last been used to warm the blanket in a basket of puppies, and to boil a kettle and fill it. We pressed it against her chilly ankles. We both begged her to let us call the doctor, but even Charlie couldn't persuade her. 'I simply have a cold. If you would be kind enough to bring me a couple of aspirin and something hot to drink, I will soon be better. I have a horror of doctors, and of hospitals.'

'All right. But let us take Prudence again, just for today, Miss Featherstone,' said Charlie.

'Thank you. Please call me Honoria. It is my given name,' said Miss Featherstone.

'We are honoured,' said Charlie. He had always had a wonderful way with Miss Featherstone, and now accepted her invitation with exactly the right words.

'I am afraid I am not as spry as I used to be. It had to come, it is in the nature of things. What I am really worried about is Prudence. Supposing it reaches a point when I am unable to care for her properly? If she were an old dog, I would have her put down. But she is only six, and she is in good health, She has her life before her.'

'Well,' I said, striving to be funny. 'She did at least see life with Fang.'

Honoria's chuckle led to a horrible fit of coughing, followed by vomiting. We washed her face. After that, Charlie pointed out to me that it would be irresponsible, indeed criminal, if we did not get a doctor.

By the time the doctor arrived, Honoria Featherstone was dead. Leaving him to cope, I put Prudence under my arm and walked away. Charlie would never mow her lawn again. I hoped she had heard me say, before she finally lost consciousness, that we would take care of Prudence.

At supper, we spoke of Honoria Featherstone. 'You know,' said Charlie, 'it's almost lucky she died just now. She might have regretted asking us to tu-toi her if she had got better.' That night, we allowed Prudence to sleep in our bedroom.

The nephew appeared, and made arrangements for the funeral, which was lavishly attended. He had obtained the services of the very best undertakers. One of their functions was the provision of a book to be signed by those attending. It was conveniently positioned beside the plate provided for offerings. I took a good look at it later. Some of the signatures were ancient and quivering, a few so grand as to be defined only as Reculver, Lanark and other indications of ancient dukedom. I would never now discover whether or not any of these ancient aristocrats might once have been suitors for the hand of Honoria Featherstone in her long-ago youth. How little I knew about her.

Those who gave full names were Colonel Patterson (the letters that followed the signature were difficult to identify), Mr and Mrs Bernard Simpson and then, far down, Charles and Annie Finlay.

At the post-funeral reception, there was good champagne. This had been provided for years ago in Miss Featherstone's will, and was one thing I did learn about her from the nephew. I didn't learn much else, save

136

that she had, he said vaguely, 'done something in the war'.

The only other thing I gathered was that the house was to be sold. Although it had been in the family for generations, it was now so decrepit that it would cost countless thousands to make it fit for the nephew, his wife and their family to live in, much as they regretted having to part with it.

The subject of Prudence's welfare arose. There was no question of the Simpsons taking her. I rather feared that they were hard pressed to maintain their affection for Flip and Flop now that their patronage of Miss Featherstone had been concluded by the grim reaper.

I was in the middle of announcing that we intended to look after Prudence when Bill Patterson stepped forward and addressed the nephew. 'I'll take the dog,' he announced. The nephew immediately told him how very good it was of him. I could already see the makings of the next OLD SOLDIER piece in the Parish Magazine, as he responded, 'Don't worry, I'm pretty good with dogs. And in any case, it will be a therapy for my wife, who has, poor dear, little to occupy her these days, with the girls grown up. She is somewhat under the weather.'

Only later did I learn that it was at this time that Margaret's chief preoccupation was planning to leave her husband. Prudence, who took to her as warmly as Fang had done, had no idea that she was coming between Margaret Patterson and freedom.

25

The Simpsons now put their house on the market at three hundred thousand, sold it immediately and bought Miss Featherstone's old home for two hundred thousand. This transaction at least aroused some interest in Jenny.

'You know what?' she said to me, 'Pigott's are furious.' Pigott's was the appropriate name of the estate agent's where Jenny had had such unhappy experiences.

'Why are they furious?' I asked. 'They sold the Simpsons' house.'

'Yes, but Miss Featherstone's nephew sold direct to the Simpsons, no agent.'

In spite of being totally run-down, Miss Featherstone's house was still capable of being restored to its former grandeur. Tess and Bernard Simpson were now 'Lord and Lady of the Manor' Tom told me scornfully, digging out a clump of Michaelmas daisies which had not done well. Tom had no time for slackers.

This advance of the Simpsons' life took place with remarkable rapidity. Miss Featherstone's ancestral home had had the unremarkable name of The White House. The Simpsons now renamed it Featherstone Place, claiming that that was what it had once been, and should be again, in Miss Featherstone's memory. Tom said he had never heard it called anything else but The White House, and added 'Bad luck, that, renaming a place. Like ships. It doesn't do.' We all laughed.

About this time the girl who had taken over Jenny's job at the Casuarina Tree suddenly walked out.

'Well really!' said Dick. 'She didn't even give notice, never mind clear her tables. Still, just as well, really. She never had Jenny's touch with the customers, quite the opposite; downright rude, sometimes. Really hurt people's feelings. We're glad to be shot of her, though we'd never have dared to fire her, she was the suing sort. Even so, we're a bit pushed, now, with no waitress at all.'

I saw my opportunity and took it. I put it to Jenny that she was really needed. My timing was right. She was frightened of her father but nevertheless aware that he didn't care a damn what she did with herself. And she had little real contact with her mother. All that Margaret was doing was to take longer and longer walks with Prudence, and then retire to her room.

Jenny was too fat to wear her previous restaurant outfit. I happened to have a Laura Ashley which I was happy to be able to tell her was too young for me, and would give her the pretty look that the Casuarina customers would like. 'They always loved you, Jenny.'

Dick and Desmond were delighted to have Jenny back, and soon set to work to make her over. Between them, they got her hair shaped and shampooed, and spent their own money on a lavish collection of Lancome for her face.

Bill Patterson had in his own words, washed his hands of his younger daughter. Jenny's wilful return to her degrading job was the last straw. In any case, he was completely busy with his own local importance.

The Simpsons flatteringly accepted his advice on the doing up of Featherstone Place. In fact, Bill was as much absorbed in this as he was in his connection with the Parish Magazine. The best thing to be said of him was that he was quite practical when it came to such things as central heating, plumbing and electricity.

139

I can't say that Jenny was actually happy, but she was, thank goodness, busy. Dick and Desmond, that bustling pair of masterminders, ran her off her feet.

I now saw quite a lot of Florence. She was working on moving into Peter's place. Her manner of going about it was to prepare healthy vegetarian meals and take them over, with bottles of organic apple juice. I learnt from her more than I needed to know about the virtues of foods that sounded to me as though they would make good compost.

Peter had become very distant with me. My work went through rapidly and unquestioned, and I got on quite well with Carl, who had now decided that I was wonderful, in spite of my advanced years. I relished all this on a day by day basis and, having no problems, had no need to approach Peter.

Then one afternoon I was working when Peter arrived in my room. I think he had had a considerable lunch. 'How is Jenny?' he asked.

'Absolutely fine,' I said. 'She's looking great.' This was as far as I would go in 'serving Peter right'. I couldn't help still being fond of him, and I knew Jenny had sought the relationship. But, even so, he was, or should have been, the more grown-up of the two of them.

'I'm sorry about it, Annie, I really am. I didn't think she would get so fond of me. I only thought she'd had a rotten beginning to her sex life, and I could do something about it. And she did enjoy it, being made love to, I mean. And you see, she's so pretty, the sort of girl who's a honeypot. I just thought she'd have a nice time with me for a while and then, when the time came, marry anyone she chose.'

'I don't think Jenny saw it quite like that.'

'Oh, Annie, what a mess I've made of everything.'

There seemed little point in my going on about it. So I

140

just said 'Well, you are a bit drunk at the moment, so you're sorry for yourself. But you can't say you've made a mess of *everything*. You've done very well with this agency, and you've given me gainful employment just at the right time in every way. So will you shut up and go home before you make an ass of yourself.'

'Florence will be there, treading the tofu.'

'That,' I replied, 'is your problem, you blithering idiot.'

I was absolutely determined that Jenny should hear nothing of Florence's onslaught. She was sensitive, not only the possessor of a loving heart but also deeply, passionately, lastingly, in love. She had forbidden herself to cling to Peter, and had come home, not so much to lick her wounds but more to struggle to conceal them from an unsupportive family.

I was glad to see that she was now losing weight. Dick and Desmond's régime forbade nibbling and I made her come swimming two or three times a week. I rather hoped to see her indulge in a good cry. When I was deserted, I had not cried, it was what you didn't do, then. But nowadays it seems that letting it all out and pouring gushes of salt water is the in-thing. Jenny did not conform in that respect.

My particular concern that she should know nothing of Florence's pursuit was because I was filled with a terrible dread that Florence might succeed in nobbling Peter. Like so many unappealing people, she had the grim determination of the underdog. I have often noticed that the tyranny of the weak is mightier than the strength of the brave. Florence was going, with Uriah Heepish relentlessness, for what she wanted. I resolved that, should Florence manage to sneak him into the registrar's office, I would murder Peter.

*　　*　　*

141

A noticeable part of Littlefold life was that one was very aware of the seasons. I had thought, during our London days, that I knew about seasons: holidays away in summer, theatres and cocktail parties in winter. But country life, and Littlefold really was pretty much what's left of country life, was where you really knew about the changing seasons. I have said it was a rainy autumn. It was now a cold one. I was more and more grateful for the warmth of our own house and the increase in my income that permitted me the luxury of continuing to heat the swimming pool without worrying about it. I refused to feel in the least guilty about owning, and thoroughly enjoying, a swimming pool. In terms of the rest of the world's sufferings, I put it with the long-ago uselessness of giving up sweets for Lent on account of children who hadn't any.

Jenny began to look attractive but, to me, strange. Under Dick and Desmond's auspices, her face assumed a lacquered appearance, the sort of mask you couldn't cry in. She did her work with efficiency, was as courteous as ever to the customers but much less chatty than she had been with them before.

It was obvious to me that she didn't want to talk about Peter. She never even asked me about my days at the agency, which was unlike her, as she had always taken a touching interest in me and my doings.

The people who bought the Simpsons' previous house had two sons who were frequently home for weekends. Anyone could see that Jenny, with her now regained figure and her elegant facial veneer, appealed greatly to both of them. But as Christmas approached, and parties began, if she went to them at all, she tended to stick to Charlie and me. Her father she ignored, and Margaret, as usual, never went to any sort of party.

26

January stumbled in. Everyone told one another that they'd had a wonderful Christmas and New Year but that they were glad it was all over. Germs were rife in the office, and I caught a cold which I generously gave to Charlie.

Florence with a cold was a particularly unattractive sight. She kept popping vitamins between her drooling lips in the intervals of unprotected sneezing. It worried her that she couldn't look after Peter, who was off sick with what Florence called a 'fluey cold'. I told her tartly, 'There's no such thing as a fluey cold. You have a cold, or you have flu. They are not the same thing at all.'

Colds, usually elevated to the status of flu, swept Littlefold. The Simpsons went down. I was weak enough to go and take Flip and Flop for walks.

Bill Patterson gamely went about 'not giving in'. He sneezed in the shop, he sneezed in church, he sneezed and coughed in every possible enclosed venue.

Tom announced that he would stay outdoors, have a bonfire, cut back the clematis and leave the rose-pruning until just before Grand National Day. Tom did not catch a cold.

Margaret avoided catching her husband's bug. No doubt it was something to do with sleeping in separate rooms, long walks in the fresh air with Prudence, and remaining in her own private sanctum for the rest of the time.

In February we began to see a few snowdrops in the garden. Charlie and I had got over our colds and were feeling more cheerful.

The Simpsons went off to Barbados for sunshine. Flip and Flop went into kennels. Featherstone Place was full of builders and decorators but dear Bill Patterson, Tess informed me, had undertaken to oversee them. I wondered how the builders would respond to barked orders and, rather meanly, if they would mutiny.

At this point, Margaret decided to go and spend a week with her mother. She took the trouble to come and see me to tell me about it. 'What about Prudence?' I asked. 'Will Bill take her for walks? He's so busy looking after the Simpsons' house.'

'Bill? You must be joking. I'm taking Prudence with me.'

'To your mother's flat? What will she say? It's so elegant.'

'Actually, it was my mother who suggested I should bring Prudence. You see, I get on quite well with her on my own. Her bark's worse than her bite, and I'd rather be there than at home.' I could quite believe this sadly-given confession. The sole company of her husband and her very unhappy daughter must have been a shade depressing.

Although I say 'unhappy daughter', most people would have judged Jenny to be perfectly happy at this time. I had seen her in the restaurant, always smiling and laughing. When she came to swim, I noticed that she was now getting almost too slim. She no longer used Sally's old swimsuit, and she no longer plopped into the pool in her own skin. She now had one of those very slick suits, with a sort of harness-shaped top and very little at the bottom. 'You ought to get one, Annie,' she advised.

'Thank you, dearie, but no thanks. I'll stick to my old leotard and hide my wrinkles.'

'Charlie doesn't think you're wrinkled. You're very lucky, Annie.' This was true but I still wasn't about to tell Jenny that it hadn't always been the case. Jenny was a long way off being ready for parables, and especially parables that could only seem apocryphal to one in her brittle state of mind.

We were swimming one day when she suddenly backed up against the side of the pool and said, 'Annie, something's worrying me.' I luckily didn't say 'Peter?' as she then continued, 'My mother.'

'She's at your grandmother's, isn't she?'

'Yes, she is. And Annie, I thought I'd tidy up her room while she was away. You know, see it wasn't dusty. Put clean sheets on the bed. See if she needed any washing done. I wanted to make it nice for her when she comes home.'

'What a kind girl you are, Jenny,' I said.

'Yes, but there was a frock on the back of a chair. So I shook it out and went to hang it in the wardrobe. And there were two empty brandy bottles in there, and three empty wine bottles.'

What a fool, I thought, to go away and leave that sort of condemning evidence behind. I had never felt sadder. Not only did it seem certain that the beastly gossip must be true but also that Margaret was getting careless. I didn't feel in the least sorry for Bill Patterson. That man, in my opinion, was enough to drive anyone to drink. 'What are you going to do?' I asked. 'Are you going to discuss it with your father.'

'Certainly not, I hate my father. It's all his fault.' It certainly was, but the actual facts of that I was only to discover later.

'Jenny,' I said, 'I'll come over with a rubbish bag and we'll chuck them all in our dustbin.' We were able to carry out our raid straight away.

The next day was Thursday, my working day. When I got in, Carl was waiting for me with a pile of queries. 'Peter's still at home, off sick,' he said, 'and I've only got you to turn to.'

'How sweetly put,' I said. Carl didn't blush.

'He's ill,' mourned Florence. 'He really is. He won't let even me come near him. And I'm his best friend.'

I decided that this was the moment at which I had to have a little talk with Peter, ready or not. I rang Charlie and said, 'Don't meet the train, I may be late home. I'll take a taxi.'

'Rich bitch,' said my loving husband, and rang off.

I found Peter in pyjamas and dressing gown, unshaven. It was 3.30, a time of day I know to be dismal when one's spirits are low. 'Why aren't you at work?' I asked him.

'They can manage perfectly well without me,' he replied. 'What brings you here?'

I came straight to the point. 'What,' I asked, 'would you do if you were an unhappy young woman with an unpleasant father and an alcoholic mother?'

'I presume you're talking about Jenny. If so, from what little I've seen of them, I would agree the unpleasant father. But I do not believe that Mrs Patterson is an alcoholic. A very wretched woman, yes, but not, from what I know of such things, a lush. I haven't worked in this business for twenty five years without knowing a piss-artist when I see one. It's a tendency I watch out for in myself. Talking of which, would you like a cup of tea?' I said yes to tea, and Peter went on, 'Nettle, peppermint, lemon ginger?'

'Haven't you got any Lyons Red Label?' I enquired.

'Yes, if I go to the back of the cupboard.'

'Florence?' I asked, following him into the kitchen as he fought his way through packets of nasty herbs to find us a tea fit for real people to drink.

146

'Yes,' he said. I threw all the powdered hay into the rubbish bucket without asking his permission. We drank our tea and Peter accepted one of my cigarettes. We sat on until Peter said, 'Will you stay and have a drink before you catch your train?'

I said, 'Yes, if you will pay me the compliment of getting out of your night attire, in which you do not look like Noel Coward.'

Peter disappeared and returned in a while looking a great deal better. In his honour, I decided that the least I could do was to tidy my face up a bit. 'May I use the bathroom?' I asked.

Once in the bathroom, I reverted instantly and shamelessly to my old vice, and opened the door of the bathroom cabinet. My heart lurched as I discovered memorabilia of Jenny. Half a 28-day strip of the pill (I was morally certain this had nothing to do with Florence and that she hadn't moved in to this extent) a deodorant, and I was all too aware that Florence eschewed deodorants, and some Tampax. It wouldn't have surprised me to learn that Florence used washable, save the trees, strips of linen sheets.

Now that Peter was dressed, he asked, 'Would you like dinner, Annie? There's nothing fit to eat here, since Jenny left. But we could go out.'

'No,' I said, 'thank you, I'd rather get home. Charlie misses me. That's why I only come to work on separate days. He hates to sleep without me.'

'Charlie is your darling,' said Peter. 'Lucky him.'

'You don't know the half of it,' I replied, and then added, 'Are you going to give up advertising?'

'No, I don't think so. Florence keeps begging me to go with her to Wales and grow organic vegetables.'

'So. Florence. So what?'

'So nothing. Annie, is Jenny all right?'

147

'Jenny,' I said, 'is looking incredibly attractive. She is as slim as a wand, and her friends Dick and Desmond have masterminded her face. She is looking fabulous.'

'Not pale lipstick outlined with dark?'

'Yes.'

'She hasn't had that crooked little tooth fixed, has she?'

'No. She hasn't.'

'That I couldn't endure.'

I have never heard love declared in a less sentimental way.

27

When Margaret returned from her visit to Mrs Wallingford, she told me that her mother was reasonably well, but a little slower on the move than before. 'She liked Prudence, and luckily so did Barbara.' Barbara, it seemed, was the name of Mrs Wallingford's housekeeper, whom I had not met, as she had been away on holiday at the time of my visit.

'Jenny missed you, I think,' I said, and added, 'She does love you, you know. She spent quite a lot of time seeing that your bedroom was in order.'

'It looked very nice,' said Margaret. I did not probe. The sad collection of hidden bottles was long gone with the dustmen, from my own house, unnoticed I imagined, among quite a few of our own.

I was worried about Margaret but then something else occurred to take my attention. My friend Peter was under threat, although he didn't seem to realise it, being in a vague frame of mind, from a power-seeker.

Carl, who was determined to hit top before he was thirty, was showing signs of seeking accession to the board of directors. And it seemed that ancient Annie was destined, in his plan, to become the St Christopher-like shoulder which was to carry him across the river. My function, it appeared, was to oust Peter, and become, myself, the creative director. I had a few objections to this notion, apart from my loyalty to Peter. I did not want the job, I was far too old for it, and I had absolutely no intention of extending my two days a week by as much as two hours. I encapsulated these thoughts merely by saying, 'Are you out of your mind?'

'Oh, I wouldn't need you for very long,' said Carl, with touching naivety. 'Only as a stop-gap.' Then, perhaps realising that this could have been better put, he went on to say, 'You've been a marvellous influence. We all think your copy is quite wonderful.' And he went on to add more fulsome phrases, so clear in his own mind about what it was *he* was after that he seriously believed he could pull the old trick of flattering a silly woman into walking straight into the shit.

Fortunately, it seemed that Florence's schemes in connection with Peter had had one good effect. He reappeared in the office and re-took the control he had been letting slip of late. From my point of view, this was a great relief. Had he remained skulking in his pyjamas for much longer, there was no knowing with what speed Carl would have grasped the opportunity. And that would have meant the end of my profitable, easily handled and very enjoyable job.

There was a certain faction in Littlefold that wondered how I could bear to go up to horrible London twice a week. 'Especially in Spring. Spring is so lovely here.' That was perfectly true, but Spring, for me, was pretty nice in London, town of parks and window boxes. I had little time to spare in my lunch breaks, but such walk-outs as I took were a constant refreshment.

Littlefold was indeed all beauty but not, in my immediate circle, all jollity. At the agency, everyone lived on crises, quarrels and back-biting, but stress was not really a word to be used in connection with them. Rather, they thrived on it. For stress, I only had to look at Jenny and her mother.

I sometimes met Margaret out walking Prudence. She

always seemed pleased to see me, though she said very little. Whatever time of day I met her, I could see that she was always tense, as taut as a fiddle-string, but she showed absolutely no signs of drunkenness. When I over-indulge, I get eloquent, carried away by my own wit and not infrequently amorous. Margaret was always quiet, always steady in her walk.

Dick and Desmond reported that Jenny had actually snapped 'Make up your mind,' at some dithering customer whom she had always, in the past, taken step by step, price by price, through the menu. She had then apologised and burst into tears.

'It's so unlike her. She looks wonderful, her maquillage is perfect, she's slim. She ought to be the happiest girl in the world. What on earth's the matter with her?'

'Love,' I said.

Tess and Bernard Simpson were pretty stressed, too. Flip and Flop had brought fleas back from the kennels, and Featherstone Place had two bathrooms with dripping taps, the wrong tiles, and bidets put in back to front.

There were times when I really wanted to smack Peter. He had broken Jenny's heart, and then allowed tedious Florence to encroach to a dangerous extent. But I had to content myself with being thankful that he was now doing the job for which he was well able, with the decisiveness he had gained over the years.

When I spoke of all this, including Carl's plotting, to Charlie, he responded with, 'You never know your luck. Maybe Florence will transfer her affections to Carl. Serve him right if she makes *him* go organic in Wales.'

'Not Carl, not in a fit,' I said. 'But I do worry about Jenny.'

'You worry about everybody. Honestly, darling, I sometimes think it's a mercy we didn't have children ourselves.

You would have been a basket case before we'd got them into college.'

Bill Patterson continued to stride about the village in his soldierly way. When anyone enquired after Margaret, he would clear a worried frown from his face, replace it with a brave smile and reply that she was 'Not too grand, has her ups and downs, good days and bad.'

Having had Margaret's secret forced upon me, I had a horrible feeling. It was rather like knowing that a friend has terminal cancer and wondering whether *she* knows anything about it, and then not daring to speak of it. I couldn't bring myself to ask Jenny anything. I could only hope she would come to me whenever she needed me.

I turned, as I always do, to Charlie. His advice, as I knew perfectly well it would be, was to mind my own business. I took the advice (there wasn't much alternative) only saying rather sourly to my dear husband, 'I didn't marry Mr Right. I married Mr I'm Always Right.'

28

The day that Bill Patterson dropped down dead in front of his wife came as a great shock to everyone in Littlefold.

I was very sorry for Margaret, but only because she held herself to blame for what happened. Well, she was, when it came to the crunch. But, as I said to Charlie, 'He started it.'

Littlefold was absolutely astonished by the sudden demise, from a heart attack, of a figure they now regarded as popular. 'He was quite a young man,' mourned those to whom an under-sixty was a mere boy.

The church was full for the funeral, after which Bill's coffin was taken to the crematorium, accompanied by a number of locals as well as his widow, his two daughters and his son-in-law. I couldn't help wondering if Bill was annoyed that he didn't warrant a place in the churchyard.

I asked Margaret if she would like me to help her and Jenny to prepare the post-funeral reception that was always expected in the relict's home. To my surprise, she replied, 'I'm not giving one. If Sally and Jenny want to do anything, they can. But I've had enough as it is. I can't take any more rubbish.'

In the end, the customary reception *was* given chez Patterson. Jenny remained stony-faced throughout. 'Hard,' I heard whispered. Sally wept and told everyone how she had adored her father. Then, choking back her tears, she said in tones of sad pity, 'I'm afraid my poor mother has had to go and lie down. She's taken it very badly and, you know, she's often not very well.' At least this time there were no whispers. I don't think anyone, even Tess Simpson, would quite have had the social gall to murmur 'Drunk again'.

By now I had heard the most extraordinary story from Margaret. Certainly I had never liked her husband. But at worst I had believed him merely to be pompous, conceited and tacitly disloyal to Margaret. On the other hand, since the damning evidence that Jenny and I had concealed, I had been forced to believe that Margaret was a secret drinker and, no matter what had driven her to it, it had to be admitted that that sort of thing was very hard on a man.

As soon as I heard of Bill's death, I decided I must go to Margaret. Since he had collapsed on a Wednesday and died later in the day in hospital, I was obliged to telephone Peter and tell him that I would be unable to come to work on the Thursday. By now it was very late, so I rang him at his flat. 'Of course,' he said, on hearing the reason for my unusual defection. 'I'm so glad Jenny has you to comfort her. Poor darling, how sad for her.'

'She wasn't very fond of him,' I felt obliged to say.

'Even so, it must have come as a shock, and she's very tender-hearted. Is she all right?' I could hardly say that Jenny couldn't care less about her father's death, so I left it, that, secretly pleased by Peter's concern.

When I arrived at the house, Margaret opened the door and led the way straight into the sitting room. I had hardly seen her in there for months on end. I had also seldom seen her so well-turned-out. On occasions when I met her walking Prudence, she was usually either in wellies or clumping walking shoes, according to weather, baggy tweed skirt and anorak. And, on the rare occasions when I invaded the bedroom in which she hid out, more often than not she was in dressing gown and battered

154

slippers. 'You are brave, Margaret,' I said. 'You look splendid.'

'Jenny has taken Prudence out for me. So I tidied myself up and prepared to repel boarders.'

'Not me, I hope.'

'Oh no, Annie, not you. May I offer you a glass of sherry?'

I accepted, not that I particularly wanted one, but I thought it a good idea that Margaret should be able to take a moderate drink in company. She was very composed. In fact, she insisted upon giving me some lunch. It was a cold chicken and salad. 'I'd made it for Bill's lunch yesterday,' she said with a laugh, 'but he didn't eat it. Well, he was dying.'

We ate at the kitchen table. It was a sunny day, and the kitchen was filled with light. Margaret cut bread. 'I'm sorry I've only got this beastly Olivio stuff. Bill wouldn't allow butter in the house. Poor him, perhaps he knew his heart was wonky. Rather sad, really.'

'You sound as though you are speaking of a stranger,' I said.

'I wish I was. I wish I hadn't learnt so much about him. When we were first married, I was unquestioning. I had very little confidence in myself. My mother has gone so far as to say that might be her fault to an extent. I wasn't a boy, and I wasn't even a pretty girl. At least, she now says that I was, but that she didn't think it was good for me to be told so.'

'Your father was a brigadier, wasn't he?' I asked, partly to remind myself but also because I wanted Margaret to go on talking.

'Yes. Bill was seconded to him as lieutenant, from a regiment father didn't think much of. But he was good enough for me. And then, of course, I had two little girls. When I was expecting Jenny, I prayed it was a boy. Bill

155

so wanted one. I felt guilty, even more so because I loved her so much more than I do Sally and better, I think, than if she had been a boy. I wanted a boy because Bill did, but I didn't want one for myself.'

'How come,' I asked, 'that Bill actually didn't know you are a really good, strong swimmer?'

'He only ever saw me paddling about with the children. I would only have a real swim when I was quite by myself, not even with the children, in case they should tell their father that Mummy could swim really fast, and under the water. It was not for me to be good at anything. It was my job to admire Bill. Excellence was his prerogative.' Never had I heard Margaret so eloquent. I said so, and she added, 'I was good at essays at school. Essays and swimming. Essays and swimming do not necessarily make a good officer's wife, especially not if that officer is Bill Patterson.'

'Were you ever happy?' I asked.

'No. Except once in a while with Jenny, and the one time I swam in your pool. You know, before I tried to drown myself.' I was preparing to ask more about what had occurred the day before, but there was no need. The flood-gates were open. 'Yesterday, I took Prudence for her walk in the morning. Taking a dog for a walk is a good time to think. And what I wanted clarified itself in my mind at nine forty-five precisely. I wanted a divorce. I had known for a long time that I couldn't go on living with Bill. I thought my proposition would be simple. We haven't shared a bedroom for years. Bill didn't love me, he didn't even like me. He did like Tess Simpson, who isn't, I have reason to believe, getting on too well with Bernard these days. I thought, on the whole, that he would be pleased. All Littlefold thinks I'm a drunk. Well, I do tipple a bit.' All I had seen of Margaret's tippling was the putting of a splash of vodka in the orange juice at the long-ago party, and later a few quick gulps of the marinading wine. Margaret continued, 'When I came back from visiting my mother, Jenny told me that she'd found empty bottles in my wardrobe.'

'I know she did. She and I threw them away,' I said.

'That was kind of you. I didn't know you knew anything about it, or I would have said something. It had happened before, so, as I saw it, it clearly pointed out that I was an alcoholic, and also insane. I tried to kill myself in more ways than one, including drowning.'

There was a long pause before she continued, 'Anyway, yesterday I made a pot of coffee and asked Bill to come into the sitting room. I told him I wanted a divorce. He went what I believe is nowadays called ballistic. But I dare say I've got the word wrong. In short, he was very, very angry. "After all I've done for you?" he actually said, well, screamed is more like it. His anger had always frightened me before. But suddenly, I wasn't afraid.'

'For the first time?' I asked.

'Yes. And it was more than that. I hardly know what came over me, but it was like a revelation. I knew. I knew beyond a shadow of doubt that I had not been drinking in secret and hiding empty bottles in my wardrobe. Annie, have you heard the description "control-freak"?'

'Frequently,' I said, 'where I work the phrase is bandied about quite freely. Usually to describe account executives who've got above themselves.'

'At work is one thing. At home is another. It's taken me years of always believing myself to be foolish and wrong to find out that I had married one.'

'But what about the bottles?' I asked.

'The bottles. Oh yes, the bottles. I said to him, Bill, I take it you had some strange reason for wanting to prove I was mad. But isn't concealing empty bottles in my wardrobe going just a little too far?'

When Margaret continued to give me Bill's response to this, I could only think that it would have been comical if it hadn't been so unbelievably awful. Obviously, every word of her late husband's diatribe was permanently etched on her memory. Her voice almost sounded like Bill's as she quoted him. ' "You have been a complete failure as a wife to me. I have had too much to put up with. You have caused me so much distress that I have occasionally had a little more to drink than is good for me." So I said, "And hide the bottles in *my* wardrobe?" ' Then she returned to Bill's voice, as she again quoted him saying, ' "Well, what does it matter. I have a position to keep up and you do not. People might have seen me at the bottle bank.' I asked him if he knew I had actually tried to drown myself. He said he had suspected it but was quite glad I hadn't succeeded. I can see why. If I had died while my mother was still alive, he wouldn't get a penny. She's quite rich, you know.'

I think what I found most extraordinary was the calm, practical, almost clinical way in which Margaret related all this. Had she been hysterical or shown the usual signs of bitterness it would have been less credible. The whole saga of Bill Patterson fell into place, and I could only believe every word of it. All those times when Margaret had fallen and hurt herself, and when she had injured herself again in order to hide out in what was, to me, a pretty unsympathetic hospital environment, became more and more significant.

'So then,' said Margaret, 'I told him I was going to divorce him. He said I could do no such thing, as he was going to divorce me on the grounds of my mental cruelty. He said, "Everyone in Littlefold already knows that you are mentally unstable." It was then that I hit him. And that, I suppose, is what brought on the heart attack. So I suppose I am a murderer.'

After the funeral, while Sally was busily entertaining what seemed like the whole of Littlefold in the sitting room, I beckoned to Jenny and got her to come with me up to her mother's room.

Only with the two of us sitting, one each side of her on the bed, our arms round her, did she at last break down. 'What hurts me the most,' she wept, 'is that all those people, some of them really quite nice people, only believe what that bloody ridiculous little man would have them believe about me.'

29

'I'm not surprised she's decided to leave,' said Tess Simpson, when the news went round Littlefold that Margaret was putting her house on the market and going to Eastbourne to look after her allegedly now very frail mother.

Winter was approaching, not the best time for selling a country village house to incomers such as the Simpsons had been. So the house remained, for the time being, on the market.

With her mother and the pug departed, I hated to see Jenny rattling round in an empty house which had never been the cheeriest of places. And I wasn't in the least surprised that Sally and her husband, to whom Margaret would have given it with a pound of tea, decided against it. I couldn't have cared less about them but I did care about Jenny. So I made her move out and come to us. 'I'd be in the way,' she said.

'Well, you would be, if it was for too long. But it's only until you get a place of your own, and a job that will earn you more than you get at the Casuarina Tree.'

Jenny hadn't been with us for very long before Tess Simpson, meeting me in the High Street, told me with a sweet smile, 'Charlie seems to be very fond of that little Patterson girl. I hope you're not going to regret taking her in.' It turned out that she had seen them giggling together in the supermarket where everybody went for their main shopping, to the chagrin of the village shop.

'I hear,' I told Charlie that evening, 'that you and Jenny are having a red hot affair, while I toil at my desk in London.' We were at the table, eating lasagna and salad made by Jenny.

'You're confronting us,' said Jenny, with the first real laugh I had heard from her in a very long time.

'The ubiquitous Tess Simpson, I take it,' said Charlie. 'Well, in all fairness, she did see me in our pretty Jenny's arms in the car park.' Charlie's back had been giving him a few days of gyp, so Jenny had taken to driving him about in her own very small car, a kindness which entailed hauling him out of the passenger seat.

Although I knew I really ought to be encouraging Jenny to strike out on her own, I began, guiltily, to hope that that wouldn't happen too soon. Her cooking was a great addition to our ménage. Charlie, who had done his best since I had been so busy, had really got bored with what was not his *métier*, and we had been having too many so-called convenience foods.

Charlie, wrestling with one of these offerings, roared, 'Plastic. There's no need to worry about what we'll die of. It will be starvation from not being able to get any food out of its wrappings. If only someone would discover that there's a plastic tree, and save it.' It wasn't only Jenny's cooking. 'Youth about the house,' said Charlie, putting his arm round me, 'is very enlivening.'

I wondered whether, on the evenings when I returned after my working days, if Jenny would ever mention or ask about Peter. She never did. I liked to think she was a bit happier now that she was staying with us, and she did seem less brittle. She was still slim, and she still took care of her face but with less of the make-up that had made such a mask of that pretty feature.

One day she drove over to Eastbourne to see her mother. 'Mummy's very well,' she reported, 'and so is

Granny. Poor Granny, though, she's a bit past it now, she didn't even tell me off for calling her Granny rather than Grandmother. And she adores Prudence. Mummy's got her a wheel-chair, and she takes her along the front for Prudence's walk. Prudence always rides in the chair, on Granny's lap. I'm so glad my father's dead.'

'Jenny.' I rebuked her.

'Well, I am. He was beastly to my mother for years, and to me. But that didn't matter, I'm tough. It was Mummy I always worried about. His bloody ego. He almost succeeded in driving her mad, you know. I saw it. Do you wonder I'm glad he's dead? Imagine having a father who would do a thing like hide empty bottles in your mother's wardrobe.'

'I have heard of that sort of thing before,' said Charlie, 'I don't know psychiatric terms, and I don't pretend to. But I have heard of a sort of madness where the person can only exist by imputing his own behaviour to someone else. He probably couldn't help it. He may not even have known he was doing it.'

'He knew well enough,' I said. 'I remember every word poor Margaret told me afterwards.' In one way, I knew I shouldn't encourage Jenny to dwell on what was over and done with but it couldn't be helped; I had to say it. 'He was, quite simply, convinced that it mattered nothing if Margaret believed herself to be an insane alcoholic, or if anyone else believed it, come to that. All that mattered to him was his own conceit and his own public image.'

'I'll tell you something else,' said Jenny. 'Something I'd forgotten about until now. Once, when I was very little, I had a terribly sore face. It was all bruised black and blue. I had been pushed downstairs. Mummy was in tears, telling me how sorry she was for what she must have done to me. Yet really I knew who had done it. I knew

162

but I didn't believe myself. Maybe one day I'll tell her about it, and maybe I won't.'

Charlie and I agreed with each other that Jenny had become astonishingly mature of late, and a delightful companion. Charlie said, 'It's as good as having a pretty daughter without having to go through nappies and teething and adolescent tantrums.'

We were mildly pleased when Jenny went so far as to go out once or twice with Johnny Raven, one of the sons of the new people in the Simpsons' previous house. On the second occasion, Charlie insisted on staying up until she got home, in spite of my saying, 'Really darling, she's a grown woman, you've said so yourself.'

Jenny was obligingly open. 'We went to Canterbury, to see a play at the Marlow.'

'Was it a good play?' I asked.

'Not bad,' she said.

'Nice evening?'

'Not bad.' So Johnny Raven was not setting her world on fire.

At the Casuarina Tree, Jenny was perceived once more as her old self, kind and friendly. Her popularity was restored. But even there, changes were coming. Dick and Desmond, for so long the mainstay of the place, now decided that what they really wanted was to have a restaurant of their own.

'Of course,' they said, 'we'd have it well away from the CT. Not even in the same town. But, tell you what, we'd go for the same sort of customers. We know so much about them. We're marvellous with oldies, you see.' They were, that was true.

'What are you going to call it?' asked Charlie, 'The Oldie?'

'No,' said Dick, 'clever Desmond's thought of a wonderful name. And not The Gay Gourmet, either. It's The

163

Best Of British. They'll flock, believe me, absolutely flock. Especially when some p.c. busybody forbids us to call it that. And we'll serve lots of local food, lamb and pork and so on. And vegetables. Lovely fresh greens, and carrots and parsnips. You know, nursery-cum-golf-club food at its very best. Englishness personified.'

'What about wines?' asked Charlie, the practical. 'You'll have to import those.'

'No,' said Desmond, 'we won't. One of our best wheezes, they do it in Australia. BYO.'

'What's that?' asked Jenny.

'Bring your own. You wouldn't have heard of it, a child like you. I don't suppose you've ever even heard of the Empire.'

'Yes, I have,' said Jenny defensively. And I've heard of BYO, too, now I come to think of it. Gavin, or Gareth, whatever his name was. You know, Annie, that Australian boy you had staying, he said how awful it was that restaurants in Britain didn't do it. It's a jolly good idea. They'll love it. You know what a fuss they make at the CT about the price of a carafe.'

'And,' added Dick or Desmond, 'it will mean that we don't have to apply for a licence, and better still, we don't have to put a lot of money we haven't got into stocking a bar.'

'It sounds great,' said Jenny. 'When are you going to do it?'

'Next year. We can't just drop the CT now. Winter's their busiest time. Will you come in with us, Jenny?'

'I might. If you'll take me as a partner.' I was delighted to hear her sounding shrewd. 'I could put some money in.'

'Don't tell us, did your father actually leave you some money?'

'No. He dropped down dead without making a will.

164

Making a will was no part of his considerations. But whatever he had, my mother gets, and I've got a rich grandmother. All right then, let's talk business next year.' I thought, my goodness me, she has grown up.

Although Jenny never mentioned Peter, the same was not true the other way round. At this point, Peter never stopped working, and had imposed on himself an austerity which precluded long lunches, sharpened up the creative department and showed every sign of putting Carl back in his box.

Florence still hung in grimly, but it gradually became clear to me that she was wasting her time.

As he passed along the creative corridor, giving everyone hell, Peter's occasional resting place was my little room. He permitted himself to say, 'How is Jenny?'

'Very well,' I told him, 'and very interested in a new project.'

'I'm glad.' He didn't sound very glad. Then came the day when he quite suddenly asked me, 'Annie, would it be an awful cheek if I asked if I could come to you for Christmas.' He obviously saw that he had taken me completely by surprise. 'I'm lonely,' he added. 'Nothing's much fun.'

'I don't know whether you realise that Jenny is living with us now. What about her feelings?' I asked. I expected Peter to withdraw his request, but he didn't so I added, 'Let me talk it over with Charlie.'

Charlie was not in favour of the idea. 'I like Peter, indeed I do, and I thoroughly enjoy his company. But I'm not sure it's a good idea. I know you hate to say no. But I do suggest that you ask Jenny first.'

Jenny reacted with a calm that should have surprised me. It only didn't because I believed I had seen a new steeliness in her, particularly when she was talking business with Dick and Desmond. Now she said, 'It's your

165

house, Annie, and obviously it's for you to choose your guests.' Was this Jenny, referring to the love of her life as a guest?

As Christmas approached, Jenny's help with the preparations was invaluable. She made and froze the stuffing for the turkey. She made and froze mince pies. She found holly with berries. Charlie brought in a pretty Christmas tree. Jenny and I decorated it.

The three of us began to assemble small presents for each other, and piled them round the base of the tree. I looked in vain for anything labelled to Peter from Jenny. But only when Jenny had done everything she could to furnish the nearest thing possible to a family Christmas did she drop her bombshell.

Peter was expected before lunch on Christmas Eve. Jenny had made Coronation Chicken, and had assembled the ingredients for a fruit salad. Quite late on the afternoon before, she said, 'Annie, the fruit needs to be cut up for the salad. Best do it as near lunch time as possible. I'm going to Eastbourne.'

'Oh,' I said, 'what a good idea. Your mother will be so pleased. You'll be back for supper, I take it?'

'No. I'm staying over until after Boxing Day.' She gave no explanation of why this was the first time she had mentioned her departure, merely adding, 'Take the stuffing out of the freezer first thing tomorrow morning. It will be thawed enough to put in the turkey by evening. The mince pies are better if you put them straight into the oven from the freezer. Do it while you're dishing up the turkey.'

She ran upstairs, came down with a small case, gave me a brief hug, and was gone, having said no more.

30

If Jenny could clam up so, it seemed, could Peter. He arrived in time for lunch on Christmas Eve, shook hands with Charlie, and kissed me.

Charlie had provided an agreeable bottle of pre-prandial wine. Peter made no comment on the three glasses waiting on the tray. After lunch, he disappeared briefly and returned with wrapped packages which he put under the tree. There was a variety of parcels for Charlie and me but nothing, so far as I could see, for Jenny. I began to wonder if he had failed to take in my information that she was living with us.

During the evening, the Simpsons looked in, bearing gifts. I had not thought of getting anything for them, so did my best with over-stated thanks while Charlie offered drinks and I hastily smeared some pâté on crackers. It was too late to take out and bake some of the mince pies, unless there was to be a much longer sit-in than I could do with.

'Isn't Jenny here?' asked Tess, looking significantly at Peter.

Charlie cut in. 'She decided to go to her mother's. She was concerned about her.'

'How *is* poor Margaret?' asked Tess.

Bernard then announced that he and Tess were going to spend a Yule-log Christmas Day at a hotel a few miles away. I had the decency to anticipate the request that they perhaps might, having apparently dropped in for the sole purpose of offering presents, find it difficult to be blatant enough to make. 'Would you like us to have Flip and Flop for the day?' I asked.

I was at once told how very kind this was of me. Flip and Flop were duly delivered to us on Christmas morning. We all got great mirth out of the Simpsons' presents. Mine was a book on flower arrangement which I had seen some weeks earlier in the window of a remaindering bookshop. Charlie's was a mail-order pair of gardening gloves.

Meanwhile the Christmas Eve visit had been concluded by the arrival at our door of carol singers. It was a group from the local church, so none dug deeper into the pocket than the Simpsons, Tess going so far as to wrest a five pound note from Bernard.

Our Christmas dinner, which we ate at about three in the afternoon, went through with no mention of Jenny. We all got agreeably flown, in that slow, on-going Christmas Day fashion.

I forgot Jenny's instructions to put the mince pies in the oven, and only remembered at the Stilton and port stage. By the time I produced them, with a pot of tea, Charlie and Peter were snoring in the sitting room under tipsy paper hats. Charlie's glasses had slipped to the end of his nose, and Peter had loosened his trouser belt. 'What a pretty sight,' I said.

Somehow, up until this moment, we had forgotten all about the gifts under the tree. Charlie and I had wrapped up some pretty things for Jenny, and I had left them under the tree to await her return. There were packages from Jenny to Charlie and me, but nothing there for Peter.

We gave each other presents, tore off the wrappings and exclaimed. We went on nibbling mince pies as we finished tea, and then Charlie decided that a nice clean Scotch-and water all round would do us good.

168

Whether it did us good or not, I'm not sure. But it certainly had the loosening effect of making me respond to Peter's 'Lovely mince pies,' with 'Jenny made them.'

'Oh! Where *is* Jenny, by the way?' asked Peter, trying to sound casual, and just as though Tess Simpson had not already caused the gaff to be blown.

I said, as though the subject had not been mentioned, that she had gone to Eastbourne to see her mother, to which Charlie added, wide awake on his second whisky, 'You may as well know, Peter, she went because you were coming.'

'Did she say so?' asked Peter.

'Not in so many words. In fact, she only seemed to decide quite suddenly, but it's my belief that she had made up her mind as soon as Annie told her. You see, Annie, that's obviously why she did so much preparing ahead of time.'

'You can hardly blame her,' I said. 'After all, you ended the affair. She may very well have been slightly afraid of getting hurt again.'

'I hoped she'd be here,' said Peter, perversely.

'Well,' I said, 'I know you did. That's really why you wanted to come, wasn't it? No need to demur.'

Peter tried to laugh. 'I love you for yourselves alone. But yes, it's true. I long to see Jenny. I've been a bloody fool.'

'Would you like to go on to gin, and have a good cry?' asked Charlie sardonically.

'I don't want to have a good cry. I want Jenny. Can we go and get her?'

'You are indeed very drunk,' I said. 'Not that we aren't, as well.'

'I know. I meant tomorrow,' said Peter.

'Do you think that's wise? Or fair?' asked Charlie.

'I want her. I was a selfish brute. I didn't want the

169

responsibility of marrying a lovely girl almost young enough to be my daughter. So I told myself I was doing what was best for her. But I should have had the sense to give her what she wanted. So what? I could marry her and when I die she could marry again.'

'You,' I said, whisky-sour, 'are not only getting maudlin but silly as well. You are a very stupid man, Peter.'

'Not so stupid that I don't know what I ought to do. I ought to marry Jenny.'

Even more testily, I said, 'And so Jenny ought to marry you? Supposing she doesn't think it's such a good idea? Who do you think you are? King Cophetua? I'm sorry, Peter, the last thing in the world I want to do is to quarrel with you. But you must admit that it does sound rather as though you think Jenny has no say in the matter, and it's for you to decide what is best for her.'

'Oh Annie, you can't blame me for not thinking much of myself as a matrimonial prospect. I'm far too old, and I made a hash of it the first time round. But now, I can't help it, I just miss her all the time.'

'Look, darling,' said Charlie. 'Peter's telling us he loves Jenny, and wants to marry her. Surely it's up to him to put it to her himself, and let her decide.' He made it all sound so simple; his perennial ability to call a meeting to order was here in force.

In order to calm down, I went into the kitchen, ripped the turkey apart and made a pot of stock from the bones. There I was, fulminating against Peter's assumption that he had the divine right to decide whether or not to bestow happiness on Jenny. And who, I then asked myself, was *I* to think for her?

While certain aspects of Jenny's young life were similar to my own, I could see it was quite mistaken of me to imagine her to be a second Annie. I could well be making too much of the business acumen she had shown in

170

dealing with the restaurant proposition. But Jenny was Jenny, and I was I.

I brought the stock to the boil, clapped on the lid, and switched off the heat. We concluded the evening with Trivial Pursuit. I suggested Scrabble, but Charlie asked to be excused on the grounds of his intellect being too drunk.

I was to be glad I had dropped any argument with Peter. On Boxing Day, he showed every sign of having forgotten all that had been said the day before. We took Flip and Flop for a walk, and returned them to the Simpsons, who asked us in for gluwein, having been the only favoured Yule-log guests to whom the barman had revealed the recipe for this libation. Peter and Charlie both shuddered and said thanks, but they needed to have a swim.

I had thought that Peter had intended to return to London in the afternoon of Boxing Day. So I was surprised to see him drinking quite a lot of wine at lunch, a thing he would never have done if he had been about to drive. Even so, he made no enquiry as to when Jenny was expected back. He didn't even mention her, so neither did we.

The next morning, he came downstairs and left his packed suitcase in the hall. 'I'll go right after breakfast,' he said, 'or you'll never get rid of me. One more Charlie and Annie lunch and I'm done for.'

During breakfast, Peter went out of the room for a moment, and returned carrying a jeweller's box. 'I hadn't got round to wrapping this up, so I might as well show it to you,' he said. It was a pretty gold chain, the centrepiece of which was the name, JENNY. Memories of the ANNIE brooch given to me so long ago by Jack Davidson flooded back so forcibly that I trembled. I put the comparison away; it had nothing to do with the case.

171

The morning wore on, and I made coffee. Peter said, 'I really must get going,' and went on sitting.

In the end, I said, 'Peter, of course you're welcome to stay for lunch, but if you do, you know it's more than either Charlie or I could do to refuse you a glass or three of wine, so you really had better get on with it. Do you want to leave the necklace here for Jenny when she gets back?'

'I don't think so. She might not want it,' said Peter. 'You were probably right, and it's not for me to decide what's best for her.' Even as he picked up his case and went slowly to his car, and took forever saying goodbye, I kept hoping Jenny would appear, and thinking that I should have bitten my tongue off before I had spoken as I did on Christmas afternoon.

It was almost evening when Jenny got back. She brought messages and gifts from her mother and Mrs Wallingford. In reply to our enquiries about her Christmas, she told us, 'I'm glad I went. My grandmother says she's dying but she shows no signs of it. I have to say, my mother's a different woman. I can't tell you what it feels like to be able to talk to her without my father hanging over us.'

'Did you tell her you're thinking of going in with Dick and Desmond's restaurant idea?' Charlie asked.

'Yes, I did. She thought it would be good, and she was jolly helpful. For a start, she says she'll make the house over to me, and I can either live in it or sell it, whichever I think best. I'll have to decide. It's far too big for me on my own, so I'll probably sell it. Then I'll have some money for the business. I could get a flat or a very small cottage. I've got to live somewhere, and I can't foist myself on you forever.'

'Why not?' said Charlie. 'At least you could continue to embrace me in public and give dear Tess something to talk about.' I could see he was trying to bring a smile to

172

Jenny's face, which was exhausting itself in an effort not to look woebegone.

'Peter only left this morning. He was sorry to miss you.'

'Was he?' was all Jenny said.

31

The week between Christmas and New Year was more than usually flat in the Finlay household. There was no point in my going up to the agency for my usual two working days. Peter would be there to field anything necessary, and things would be very quiet, with many of the staff and most of our clients away skiing or sunning according to taste.

Jenny continued to talk resolutely about her plans with Dick and Desmond.

Dick and Desmond had become extremely enthusiastic and realistic, particularly as the promise of the house had made things so much more possible. My original reason for inviting Jenny to stay with us was that I didn't like to leave her alone in a large house with only distressing memories in it. But Dick and Desmond now made things seem very different.

'Why sell it?' they said, and came up with the idea of using it for their business partnership of three. 'Of course we'd never get permission to run it as a public restaurant, but there's nothing in the world to stop you from having a bed and breakfast there.'

'Sooner you than me,' I said. We were sitting round my kitchen table, and my eye lit on a pile of saucepans in the sink which Charlie had been going to wash up yesterday. The thought of paying visitors filled me with horror.

'Quite right, Annie, not your thing at all,' said Desmond. Now that they were on the verge of becoming business

174

partners with my young friend, Dick and Desmond had overcome their habit of addressing me as 'Dear Mrs Finlay.' 'But you do see,' he continued, 'what a good idea it is. We three could really make a go of it. What I thought was this. Hardly any b-and-b's give dinner, and all we'd have to do is to offer dinner if required. That way we would only have to shop to order and actually we could charge enough to offer a couple of glasses of wine without billing them. Perfectly in order, I do assure you. I found out about it.'

Jenny appeared, on the face of it, happy. But I had come to know her so well that I had developed, in spite of my elected attitude to her as a friend, not a daughter manqué, that deeper insight that only mothers are supposed to have.

Whenever, as a child, I had said I was bored, my mother's response had always been, 'Do something about it, then, or at least think of others.'

So I turned my mind to Jenny, and decided on some social life for her. 'I've got a bright idea,' I said, one dark morning. I could see Charlie trying not to listen, so I plunged on. 'Let's do something on New Year's Eve. Let's invite people. Let's have a party.'

'Anything for a quiet life,' said Charlie. 'With any luck, they'll all have arranged something already.' But he was doomed to be disappointed on that score.

The Simpsons were delighted with the idea. They were off on a cruise on New Year's Day. 'We were planning an early night,' said Bernard, in one of his rare utterances, 'but we'll be glad to make merry with you instead. Flip and Flop can go to their kennels a day early.'

The Casuarina Tree was to serve an early dinner on the night, starting at six-thirty, as most of its customers would need to totter off to bed long before midnight.

All our invitees could reach us on foot. Just as well on

Breathalyser Night Of The Year for the Constabulary. And such taxi drivers as usually came our way were always gone to earth on New Year's Eve, not caring for sick on their back seats.

The Raven family (remember them, the people who had bought the Simpsons' previous house?) accepted, including Johnny, who had not quite given up on Jenny.

Apart from the Vicar, who had to decline on account of standing in for a bell-ringer afflicted with gout, we had quite a large number of Littlefold's population.

Jenny and I got to work on the food. Charlie complained that any further depredations on our cellar would bankrupt us, and went out and bought several of those boxes with whoopee cushions full of plonk inside them. Dick and Desmond generously provided some champagne for the stroke of midnight.

The party was a success, except for Johnny Raven, who tried to kiss Jenny, and got her ear.

Much interest was shown, and enthusiasm asseverated over the Jenny/Dick/Desmond bed and breakfast scheme, 'Just what Littlefold needs.' Dick and Desmond brought the house down by inviting Jenny to marry one or other of them and give the establishment a respectable air. Jenny laughed as heartily as anyone.

She was very quiet the next morning. 'Hangover,' she explained briefly. I wished Peter had left his gift for her. As soon as she had finished not eating her breakfast she went up to her room.

Later, I went to see if she would like anything, maybe some soup. I knocked on the door, and assumed that the sound I heard meant 'come in'. It did not, it was Jenny crying. 'Jenny darling,' I said, 'don't cry. Everything's wonderful for you. You're a woman of property. You're going into business. Dick and Desmond will be very good at it, and tremendous fun. You've got so much to look forward to.'

176

'I've got nothing to look forward to,' said Jenny and continued to weep as though weeping was something she had invented and wasn't going to relinquish. 'It makes it worse, being here with you and Charlie,' she sobbed. 'You're so happy together. You always have been. You got it right.'

I had never told Jenny about my pre-Charlie life, and now was no time to break a good habit. So I hugged her, emerged exhausted and decided that getting back to work was essential to my own sanity.

I almost thought I would never get to London. The train kept stopping and eventually had a nice lie-down outside London Bridge. At last Charing Cross was reached, with the complacent intercom instructions, delivered as we at last crossed Hungerford Bridge, to remember to take all our luggage, bombs, drugs and other devices with us.

It was late indeed when I seated myself at my nerve-soothing desk and started on the accumulated pile of requisitions. I had been working, blessedly uninterrupted, for about an hour when Peter appeared. I pretended we were going to talk shop, but Peter came straight to the point. 'Annie, please tell me about Jenny.'

'She's going ahead with Dick and Desmond. They're going to turn the house into an up-market bed and break-fast.'

'And is she happy with that? Did you say anything to her about me?'

'Peter, no. It wasn't for me to interfere. She's doing her best as she sees it. But if you really want to know the truth, she's pining for you. I found her weeping in her room, and it wasn't PMT, I do assure you. It was you.'

'She doesn't have PMT,' said Peter, 'I know that. I know every little thing about her. I love her.'

'Then I suggest you do something about it, like, tell her. And I suggest that you ask her, carefully, mind, if she will forgive your earlier idiocy and marry you.'

'May I come back with you this evening?'

'No, you may not. She'd think I'd engineered it.'

'What shall I do? Shall I write her a letter?'

'You could. But I think a better idea would be to ring her up and ask her to come to your place. Maybe say she left some things behind and she might need them. Or something. You have to think it out.'

I pushed Peter out of the room, got on with my work, sent out for sandwiches, did more work and then went home to my husband and my swimming pool.

Next morning, Jenny asked me, 'Are you going to work on Thursday? Can I come up with you? I'd like to do some shopping in town, and I might stay with a friend overnight.'

On the Friday, she telephoned. 'I think I'll stay in town for a few days. If I can come back with you on your next working day, I wouldn't be a nuisance, because Charlie will be meeting you anyway.'

'Surely,' I said non-committally, 'are you having a nice time?'

'Very, thank you. There's always so much to do in London, isn't there? Theatres, art galleries, all that.'

It was a smiling Peter who came into my office to interrupt my work once again. 'Cat swallowed the cream?' I asked, and was soundly kissed. 'I see,' I said, 'cream and sugar.'

'And honey.'

'How did you do it?'

'In bed. Where else?'

'All that talk about theatres and art galleries. I hope you were careful. She was off the pill, wasn't she?'

'How do you know?'

'I saw the remains. I look in people's bathroom cupboards. A vile habit, I know. I'll give it up if you'll just tell me what Jenny said.'

'She said yes. And no, we weren't careful.'

Later in the day, Jenny arrived to pick me up. The first thing I noticed was the JENNY necklace. 'No engagement ring?' I enquired.

'No. I'm not engaged. I don't want to be engaged. Peter got engaged to his first wife and look what happened to that. We'll just get married quietly in a registry office.'

'Registrar's,' I said sententiously, 'and we'll discuss that later. Meanwhile, let's go home and tell Charlie and have a swim to cool you down.'

For the wedding, I wore a hat that knocked the eye out of Littlefold. Margaret attended bare-headed, which brought a sharp comment from Mrs Wallingford, enthroned in her wheelchair and wearing her hat like a crown. I was greatly relieved later, to hear her praising Charlie's choice of champagne. Sally, husband and sons were all present, Sally not best pleased as Jenny had refused to let the little darlings act as pages. All Littlefold was there, and so were Dick and Desmond, attired in magnificent morning suits. Jenny walked, unaccompanied, having eschewed the custom of being given away along with that of hymeneal attendants, up the aisle. As Peter's earlier marriage had been annulled, the Vicar was able to give them a marriage ceremony, and very happy the pair of them looked.

Dick and Desmond were not displeased at this new turn of events. Jenny still owns the house, they run it, highly successfully. I have no doubt that Colonel Patterson would turn in his grave or, more accurately blow his ashes, if he knew that his old home was now a commercial bed and breakfast establishment, run by a couple of gays.

Peter is still Creative Director at the agency. 'I'll have to stick it out,' he said, just as though he wasn't thoroughly enjoying his restored enthusiasm for the business he knows so well, 'so that Jenny can be a rich widow when I die.'

'Don't you dare,' said Jenny, 'I'll kill you if you do.'

I'll tell no more. I'll stop while I'm at a happy ending.

FROM
BEARWOOD
AND
BEYOND

From One Black Country
"Creative" to another

To Polarbear from the
Brummie Bard All the
best Steven

Keith Bracey

APS BOOKS
YORKSHIRE

APS Books,
The Stables, Field Lane
Aberford, West Yorkshire,
LS25 3AE

APS Books is a subsidiary of the APS Publications imprint

www.andrewsparke.com

First published worldwide by APS Books in 2023

A FEW WORDS

I am a Birmingham born and bred poet, writer and blogger who has lived in the Black Country for the last 32 years.

I came from Bearwood and went to George Dixon Academy and then Birmingham and Nottingham Universities

I worked for over 20 years for the city's former inward investment agency Locate in Birmingham, promoting my home city to international businesses.

I also project managed the relocation of the Elmhurst School for Dance from Camberley in Surrey to Edgbaston in Birmingham

to become the feeder ballet school for the Birmingham Royal Ballet.

My thanks go to Lee Benson for prompting me to put this idea of a book of poems together and for his great assistance in collating and editing these pieces for me. If he hadn't have done this, they might all be still hidden in a drawer somewhere

And finally Old Joe, the University of Birmingham clock tower is on the front of my book because the University played such a big part in my life having studied there in the 1970's and worked there from 2015 until 2020.

If you want to read more of my poetry and my blog please go to:

http://keithbracey.wordpress.com

CONTENTS

PLAYED IN BIRMINGHAM

Blues, Bears, Barons
Villains, Wasps and Wolves
Harriers, Saddlers, Bullets
Baggies, Bees and Bulls
Four football grounds to visit
Four home team strips to buy
Colourful scarves round cold necks
Or for fans to hold up high
The oval ball pulls in the crowds at Moseley RFC
For mucky rucks and scrums so tough
Such spectacular tries to see
Their followers stand together
With drinks held in their hand
They roar and sing to urge their boys
Uniting rugby in their stand
Against violence in the land
It's cricket in the summer
To Edgbaston fans will go
Watching men in white in a crease with bat
A five dayer seems oh so slow
The Twenty Twenty is much more fun
The ball flies everywhere
There are wickets, sixes and catches
As we cheer on Birmingham Bears

BLACK COUNTRY LUNGS

Twas on the day that Harry and Meghan wed
We came together to honour our Black Country dead
Those living too sharing that vital spark
That they used to light up here at lovely Lightwoods Park
Black Country lungs that breathe their last
For so many the deadly die was cast
With smoking and industrial disease
The cause of their early much lamented demise
Black Country lungs were ravaged by COPD
A blessed release as they passed, it set them free
Women like Ann told how she couldn't breathe
Her Brummie lungs congested by a Black Country
disease
Then along came Corinne to take pictures of their plight
With oxygen masks helping them make light
Of this terrible disease which was such a blight
But Corinne came along to make them feel bright
By telling their stories to the rest of the world
It gave them purpose as their suffering unfurled
Such lives well lived in the tough foundries and mines
These Black Country folk had shown such backbone and
spine
In their fight to make a livin' in tough times
Corinne Noordenbos this Dutch lady artist
Gave them their lives back with a voice at their parting
Black Country lungs breathe their last in the park
Black Country folk are the 'Salt of the Earth'

GUNPOWDER JOE

'Twas Joseph Priestley
This Lunar Man
Who discovered rushing Oxygen all around us in the air
The range of his knowledge
Was immense as a Protestant Polymath
An 'Upstart Unitarian'
But he now wanted revolution
As had happened in France
With the tumbril's wheel
Run to the ghastly guillotine
Like a shelter strewn scalpel
To exorcise the excesses
Of Louis the Sixteenth
And Marie Antoinette
'Let them eat cake'
She uttered as she was the last one to wriggle in death
From the last place on earth
Which had been her shelter: Paris La Bastille
As a King's consort in revolutionary France
Priestley also praised revolution in America
But in the Priestley riots at 'Fairhill' his home in Sparkhill
The Brummie mob bore him ill will
And 'Gunpowder Joe' was forced to flee
From his home in Sparkhill
By hook or by crook
He escaped on the run rushing to the Americas
To live out a quiet life in Maine in the USA
Where his great achievements were all but unknown and
forgotten
One of the greatest chemists and scientists the world has
ever seen

GENTLE BEN THE AMERICAN LUNAR MAN

Lunar links with the USA
Were forged by William Small
This man of math
And his type of craft
Was as a physician
He met with 'Gentle Ben'
In Birmingham
Franklin the American
Lunar Man who looked
At lightning with a
Metal conductor which
Created a lustrous lightning ball
He tried to tap with
His lightning conductor
Trying to store the
Electricity in some way
To use the power another
Day with powerful storage
And electricity became the
World's greatest source
Of Energy before it's time
In this energetic enlightenment
Begun in Birmingham
The one in the West Midlands, England
Not the one in Alabama
In the USA where revolution
Was in the air, as in France with the Lunar Men
In full support of revolution for the common man
With preacher Gunpowder Joe Priestley
Raising revolution from his pulpit
In Birmingham leading to the riots of 1791
It took another 40 years in 1832
With Attwood MP's political coup on
Newhall Hill with
30,000 men and true

The London Government
Led by Tamworth's Peel
Were scared to death
That revolution was afoot
As it had been thought in 1819 at Peterloo
Where eighteen good men so true
Were struck down by army militia
In Manchester Town
Without the British Government

Raising a frown
These 'Men of Men'
All came together from all
Around the Midlands
Wedgwood from Stoke
Erasmus from Lichfield
Samuel Galton from Great Barr
Not too far from the epicentre
Of their thoughts and ideas
At Soho House where
These Good Lunar men met
To discuss the theories
And latest science
Of the day from revolutionary France
Where chemist Antoine Lavoisier
Had paved the way for
Joseph Priestley with his
Theory of Phlogiston'
Which led to this
Revolutionary Player's
Discovery of the air of life
Oxygen; The most important gas
Along with Hydrogen which combined made
'Adam's Ale' the fount of all life, giving water to the
common man
whose lives these Lunar Men so profoundly made
Creating the modern world right here in Birmingham

It wasn't just steam power these great men meant to use,
Josiah Wedgwood created the ceramic circle in the six towns of Stoke
In what became known as 'The Potteries' up North of Birmingham
Where Samuel Galton this Quaker Slaver's man
Would sell his weapons of death
To unwary Africans on the Gold Coast
When the guns exploded in their awful faces
And their power enslaved their fellow man
Shipped to the West Indies
On death ships
Where many expired on their way across the Atlantic
To a watery grave
 Rather than face enslavement
In the Caribbean where it took until the US Civil War to free the slaves
With the Union consigning the Confederacy to defeat in 1865 under the North
Of Abe Lincoln and the Emancipation of the Slaves had been the aim of Most of the Lunar Men
The Sympathetic sorrowers
Of enslaved black men
As you see these Lunar Men improved the Lives of all
No longer were slaves left in thrall to
"Old White Men"
This Lunar Society improved the lot of all
And created the modern world
In Soho Houses' fair halls by dining together and
Sharing wine and beer and good food
This revolutionary brood of world changing wizards

THE LUNAR MEN

Well met by moonlight
These Lunar Men, these 'Men of Moment, great men all
Gave thought to science
Held nothing in their thrall
The 'Natural Philosophers'
Of the widening world
Held mostly against the enslavement of Brothers
Felt deep the pain of others
In Africa, where one of their number by name of Galton
Sold guns as a Quaker,
A real 'Wrong 'Un'
At Great Barr Hall he lived,
High on the Hog
Admonished by the other Lunar Men
Be damned in Hell for exploiting his brethren
They weren't all bad
These 'Lunarticks'
Whose ideas were thought to be full of tricks!!!!!
By ordinary men, the Brummagem mob
For when they praised revolution in France and America

The Priestley riots ensued in Brum, in 1791
'Gunpowder Joe' Mr Priestley to you
Would espouse revolution
From his fiery pulpit true
But soon Mr Priestley had to the Americas fled
Fearing for his life as the Brummie mob burned down his
home in Sparkbrook
Sparks indeed they flew
And Joe made a good life in the US too
The discoverer of O2
This Northern Lad, an adopted Brummie
Feared for his life and was forced to flee
When he did not go down on bended knee
To this Brummie mob

Who'd foam off at the mouth and shout their gob
Against the enfranchisement of the common man
In revolutionary France and the US
Where these Lunar Men continued to bless
Their thoughts and ideas
I do confess
Were 'Out of this World'
And they created this modern world
In these 'Times of Enlightenment' in the West Midlands
centred on Birmingham
And Soho House: Boulton, the 'Foremost Man'
The maker and creator of this great group
His recruitment of James Watt
His greatest coup!!!!
The Scots Engineer and gigantic genius walked down
from his home in Greenock
Down to Brum to work with Boulton; two great men
Whose ideas transformed the world into an industrious
place
This 'Green and Pleasant Land' this 'Jerusalem'
Became: 'Black by Day and Red by Night'
As coal and iron powered by Watt's steam
Transformed the Earth into this 'maker's place'
Where Boulton and Watt
Created fantastic factories to make
Their enormous great gigantic engines
Such as that from Smethwick, the last remaining in
Thinktank, lost
Not producing
The World's paid such a cost
As an industrial place
Where many men dare not show their face
As 'Wage Slaves' in this relentless Human Race
Not just in science and industry
Was the 'Lunarminaries' mark made
But also in medicine with the two foremost physicians
Withering and Darwin

Seeing how to save men from death with digitalis from the common foxglove being able to cure
The 'failure of the heart' using the drug Digitalis distilled from the 'glove' like some 'Manna from Heaven'
From far above
And Erasmus Darwin, the divine doctor and poet made men better
Through his practice of medicine
But possibly his greatest legacy was grandfathering his Grandson
And 'Greatest Scientist Ever'
One Charles Darwin
'Survival of the Fittest'
Is there no end to these great men's talents?
 By 1817 the Lunar Men's star had fallen
And they were mostly all in their grave, except for the greatest of them all,
the polymath James Watt
Who didn't shuffle off this mortal coil until 1819
But the creation of the modern world was their legacy and their greatest achievement
As we all mourn the modern world's bereavement
But hope springs eternal
And AI is the future along with makers 3D printing
Which has the ability to change the world once again
With a second Industrial revolution based on Knowledge
Begun by these great Lunar Men

A CHANCE ENCOUNTER

Back in 1822 the Chance Brothers
Came together in a fraternal pact to buy the Crown Glass
Company
in Spon Lane, Smethwick
Which was to prove an industrial powerhouse in the
future
With Chances employing over 3500 men and women in
making glass
To become a company that became World Class
With Chance designing, making and erecting the glass for
the London Crystal Palace in two years
In 1851, the year of Victoria's Great Exhibition.
Chance also glassed Pugin's Westminster political Palace
this Other Place.
Along with the glass for the American Revolutionary
White House in Pennsylvania Ave in Washington DC
By this time the largest glassmaker in the World
As their credentials to the World became unfurled
By many lucrative and successful commissions
With the firm making around 2500 lighthouses at Spon
Lane their greatest coup
Saving lives across the Oceans Blue.
These innovative optic glass lenses made Chance Bros a
Class Act
Employing without a second backward glance some men
from France
Who made the Fresnel lenses for which Chance became
so famous
Safeguarding seafarers from around the globe
From a watery grave in the depths of the Ocean
Sadly, in April 1912 a ship from Belfast steamed across
the sea and foundered on an iceberg in the North Atlantic
And all at once hundreds of people became so frantic
To avoid a watery grave near a Chance light at Cape Race
Which was the Canadian place

Which first received the SOS from the RMS Titanic
But the stricken ship could not be saved and sank in
hundreds of feet of Ocean Deep keeping the secrets that
the Ocean keeps
Of death and destruction and such panic in the North
Atlantic!
This Chance glass tale came to an end in 1981 when
Pilkington bought them out
As to the Future our Chance Trust wants to build on our
9 acres a development fit for a King
With an Inland Lighthouse as a 'Beacon for the Black
Country' where the Revolution came about
At the Soho Foundry where Boulton and Watt
Those Lunar Men made the steam engines that powered
the Industrial Revolution
Driving the cotton mills of Lancashire and pumping out
the mines
where night black coal and Cornish tin were shipped by
Georgian 'Motorways' the canals
Into Birmingham and the Industrial Revolution began
right here in the Black Country and Brummagem
A hope perchance to dream that we can achieve what we
want for our site
As we will be trying to redevelop it with all our might
To achieve our dreams to regenerate our Glassworks next
to the M5
A Chance to bring Sandwell alive and change folks'
thoughts of the Black Country from a post industrial pit
to a place for tourists, visitors and trippers
To sample our Black Country delights from bread
pudding, faggots and pays, tripe and grorty dick.
And tell the wider world, that we're not thick!
These perceptions are not cast in stone and we can
change them with our ambitious plans for industrial
archaeology and a Geopark
And UNESCO World Heritage Site in the Galton Valley
which was dug by Navvies,

11

Now a conservation area to preserve our past the heritage and history of our times
With the Black Country Living Museum and its mines and engines and forges
Telling the World that the Black Country is a place of hopes and a future based on tourism
Chance Heritage Trust has a bright future as has the Black Country
Where every man and woman can live a life that's free.

LES, MY DAD

The last time I saw you, you lay stricken in your bed
After straining your broken heart
Taken to City Hospital not far from Aston near the Gun
Quarter
Where you'd worked as a 14-year-old callow youth
Carrying the sporting guns to the Birmingham Proof
House
You'd drink away your meagre wages
From Gittens Gunmakers in The Gunmakers Arms
Where you'd drink beer until you were K - Lied
As you'd call it with your pithy turn of phrase
Football was huge for you
And your beloved Aston Villa
And you'd tek me as a 4-year-old lad
On the number 11 football special buzz
From the King's Head in Bearwood
Through Rotton Park and Summerfield
Winson Green and Handsworth and the Wood
Thence to Trinity Road in Aston, next stop Villa Park
Where we'd stand Dad and Son on the Holte End the 12th
man
To me you were the 'Harborne Tarzan'
So named after the Olympian swimmer Johnny
Weismuller
The Hollywood Tarzan as you banged in goals for the
Stonehouse Gang FC
Which later on in your shortish life caused you to limp
and falter as we climbed the Holte End steps
To the top of the terrace
One time when the Villa hosted a game in the 1966 World
Cup
 A nil all bore draw between West Germany and Sir Alf's
'Animals' The Argentines
I was lost in the Holte End but was spotted by a kindly
policeman

Who brought me to the front of the terrace
Where I saw the game from the Police command post
Returned by the policeman at the end of the game to my Dad
Les loved the Villa winning the European Cup in 1982
And then 7 years later, unlucky for some he was gone
A broken heart, it was disease that put our dear Dad at such unease
He lay stricken in bed such a big strong man 6 feet 2 and 16 stones
He'd had enough in those youngish bones
And then he was taken into City Road and one dark night
Me and Mom got a call from the West Midlands Police
And they sent a car for us in the middle of the night:
'Get here quick your Dad's not well'....
'Nothing to worry about he'll be alright'
But when Mom and I got there he'd gone 5 minutes before
Up to the Great God above through Heaven's door
Where he could cheer on the Villa
From his Elysian Fields stand
And was released from his duty to keep an eye on my bipolar Mom
Who from this wicked wide world he largely shielded
Looking after her just as he had since they married in 1952
At St Germain's Church in Edgbaston
where I was christened later on in 58
Before we moved to Bearwood to await
Les's fate 40 years on in 88
When our dear Dad passed away never spending with us another day
Love you Les: 'The Harborne Tarzan' a sporting man of Weoley
Where his Dad Wilf lived in Paganal Road in Weoley Castle
By the Stonehouse pub with whippet racing and pigeon fancying

And a pint of best Ansell's bitter
Using his sister Edna as a babysitter for us three kids
And Susan and Jean our dear younger cousins
Every Saturday night Les'd drive to Weoley
Where the men would drink so much beer and we'd drive
home without a fear
Ten pints of Ansell's Mild in our dear Dad
Which was really something quite bad
 Drink driving like there was no tomorrow
There really wasn't for us to borrow
Time against the good luck we had on the drive from
Weoley to Bearwood
Where me, Les, Dot, Rich and Gill lived in this Black
country town
Near Global Smethwick an industrial powerhouse before
its time
With great world class companies like M&B and GKN,
BIRMID and Qualcast.
Smethwick Drop Forgings, the die was cast when
Thatcher came to power
She destroyed our industry and our jobs
To turn us all into Employment Exchange yobs
Who'd loaf on street corners or sit in pubs
Drinking beer until it drugs their senses and eases their
pain
Of a life that's gone down the drain
Les was an electrician not working in a factory
Not for him the drudgery of a wage slave
Matter of factly he'd do a foreigner' and rewire someone's
house
He'd always help out and do anything for anyone
This Harborne Man a giant of a guy:
The Harborne Tarzan: My Dad the mainstay .

THE PEN IS MIGHTIER THAN THE SWORD
A Poem for the Pen Museum

Birmingham's pen trade
Was what gave literacy to the world
It gave the world the means to write
And made this great city the centre
For the spread of literacy around the Globe
With over one hundred pen makers in Brum in 1891
Men like Joseph Gillott, William MItchell
And Josiah Mason and John Hinks
Using the pen nibs made in Brum
In many different coloured Quink Inks
Joseph Gillott built the Victoria Works
Named after their great Queen
Who Birmingham had never seen
As she said like Jane Austen: 'There is something direful
in the name'
Gillott entertained the young Prince Bertie
Known to be one ever so flirty
So, the prettiest of Gillott's hundreds of maidens
Were put on show
To make the nibs while Edward skirted the factory
On Frederick Street opposite our little Pen Museum
The Albert Works so named after the Prince Consort
Albert
Like two lovers holding hands across Frederick Street
Sending personally penned royal love letters using
A Victorian Penny Black stamp
In Kidderminster's Rowland Hill's Penny Post
The Albert Works was built by William Wiley
Who worked to make a successful enterprise
With many lady workers co-ordinating their hands and
eyes
To make the nibs with many difficult dies
And with many difficult phases - rolling, blanking,
marking, and piercing

hardening, annealing and raising, scouring, grinding and
slitting
All very dangerous stages for a young girl to behold for a
pitiful wage
For twenty thousand thumping pieces of work finally at
the finish
The scouring and the grinding and then at last so long
In the past in Queen Victoria's Reign when the British
Empire ruled

Three fifths of the globe
With three quarters of everything written down in the
world
Was written down with a Birmingham made pen
An astounding fact I think you'll agree
When the British were at their apogee
And 'Old Joe' Chamberlain was in his pomp
The Father of Brum, fought the Second Boer War at the
end of Victoria's Reign
A Boer battle fought so much in vain
This 'City of a Thousand Trades'
This 'Workshop of the World'
The 'Best Led City in the Empire'
With 'Old Joe' at the Helm in 1901
The Old Queen passed
And King Edward the Seventh ascended the throne
British power continued unabated until The Great War in
1914
With Birmingham makers churning out guns and bullets
and bombs
To defeat the Hun after four long tearful years in
November 1918
The 'War to end all Wars' came to a bloody end
The First Industrial conflict fought by money and
economies
And not by the men who gave their lives that we might
live free

In Picardy and Flander's Fields, the trenches and hell holes
The Somme, Arras, Ypres and the rest all good men and true
Who gave their lives to defeat the enemy.
Led by Good King George to their doom - laden deaths
And the pen trade also 'Died a Death' after firms branched out and diversified
With the final death knell came in the 1930's
When ingenious inventor Hungarian Laszlo Biro
Made a dastardly different pen
The Blasted Biro which killed Birmingham's pen trade at a stroke
And firms decided to diversify into other areas of engineering
Like Brandauer, whose pen nibs became redundant like so many workers
They made bits for cars like the Model T Ford and Herbert Austin's Austin Seven
A Little Car 'Made in Heaven'
To give freedom to the 'Common Man'
Brum's pen trade was destroyed
And all we have now is our little museum
Be sure to come and visit us
As we showcase this forgotten trade to this wondrous world
Who can't believe that the humble pen nib was 'mightier than the sword'

BBC RADIO WM: MY FRIEND'S VOICE

BBC Radio WM is our local station
Broadcasting to the West Midlands for the nation
For local news with Louise Hancock
You can't go wrong she runs it by the clock
Three minute bulletins followed by "Make a difference "
To the Birmingham and Black Country experience
Your local presenters we have Rakeem at breakfast
The first young black man to present the show at last
We've had Phil Upton, Les Ross, Daz Hale et all
All trying to be your Brummie Breakfast pal
At 10am we have Stanchers whose so bold
 A broadcaster in the Ed Doolan mould
She has politics to tax your brains
And items so diverse as the new PM to Metro trams
At 2pm Stanchers makes way for Franksy
Or is it Foxy on a Friday?
The Main Man to the Maxi?
Franksy's been on WM forever,
He's such a big tall bloke and soooo bloomin clever!
At six in the evening Daz Hales teks the stage
With the football phone in, most fans in a rage!
The Villa, the Blues, the Baggies too
Saddlers and Wolves
Yam Yams through and through
Everyone's in Daz's phone in queue
Daz is a Wolves fan, and Mike Taylor the Villa
Not sure who Henry Liston supports?
As he's such a young fella
The night are lit up by Cazza Martin
She has us all cryin and a blartin at the diabolical
dilemma
The best presenter for me on BBC WEmma!
Straight outta retirement from Brum University, I'm yer
man
The Birmingham poet, Brummie Bard, Radio WM fan!

The greatest station in Birmingham, not forgetting the
Black Country
Louring black by day and glowing red by night!
The greatest region in the country, that's awroight!

EDGBASTON: THE HOME OF TENNIS

Edgbaston is the place
Where they serve up many an Ace
Invented by Major Harry Gem:
A game for lithe athletic men
At 8 Ampton Road: 'Fairlight'
You'd see rubber balls in flight
Men and women both
They'd hit balls with all their might
In clothing... Oh so bright!
A game played in Lilywhites
As played on a manicured lawn
In the summer of 1859
Young men and women courting
Eating, drinking, laughing
Eligible bachelors and young maidens
Playing on a mown green grass court
'Good shot sir!'... they'd shout
With many a lascivious thought
The young women they did 'Glow'
As they knocked balls to and fro
Over a rudimentary net
With strawberries and cream; you bet!
Lawn tennis started to grow
Into the game that we now all know
Fred Perry, Bunny Austin,
Ann Jones, Virginia Wade
Andy Murray and Sue Barker
Grand Slam Champions were made
Now Emma Raducanu, the teen player on the up
Proud winner of her first Grand Slam: The US Open Cup
So next time you're in Birmingham
Recall Edgbaston's major gem
And the great game that he gave us:
'Game, Set and Match: Amen!'

COMMONWEALTH PEOPLE

Commonwealth people come to Brum
To celebrate youth with sport and fun
Brummies, Villains, Bluenose too
Baggies and Saddlers, Yam Yams through and through
People are all United in their common ground
Wolves, Moors and Glassboys Pitmen rough
This region's appetite for sport has no end for us
Birmingham Moseley Rugby Club, Bournville Rugby Club
as well,
The coming rugby club at Avery Fields Sports & Events
it's said
Harborne Hockey , Bournville too Edgbaston Priory
The place for many a well served ace
With lawn tennis invented there in 1858
Edgbaston's Bear's T20 Cricket for the England women
The cricket is so very fair if you happen like me to be a
Warwickshire Bear
Rugby at Coventry where the Sky Blues played
Now it's Wasps with the Ovoid leather Ball
Coventry City were so dismayed
No longer The Ricoh Football Stadium
It's now the Coventry Building Society Arena
SISU Cov's owners were issued with a slapped up
subpoena
To the courts it went as The Sky Blues fought
To stay at their home or so they thought?
Wasps dug their well heeled rugby players heels in
After all they'd bought it
It could easily end up in a messy legal court bid!
The Sky Blues went to St Andrews where they played two
seasons
Without a home to play home games in!
Now Coventry City are back at their stadium which
staged the rugby sevens as good as the London
Palladium!

They went cap in hand to Warwick University
To build 'em a super soccer stadium
That's so fit for a wayward wandering prince!
That's William who's the Villa's Kingpin!
Chair of the FA and vital Villa fan
Historians football club do they cry from The Holte End?
As the Vile fans all bow down on bended knee to Prince William
No ordinary fan!
One day in the future he'll be "King of this Island England"
 So Birmingham hosts the Polyglot Games
The Queen's baton relay was such a great lark!
Not merely just a "Walk in the Park"!
The Baton's flying here there and everywhere, not just in England and Brum
But also to Cyprus and our Indian chums, Africa, Canada, Australia, the Caribbean too
The Baton's travelling all over this wonderful world
96000 miles it's a great long run
We staged the Games this July & August 2022
I hope to volunteer at The Aquatics Centre in Sandwell
They finished it on time so Adam Peaty beat the Commonwealth's swimmers
Not just breaststroke but medley relays too!
And Dear Tommy Daley swims, dives and knits at the same time what a sport
So Brummagem's Commonwealth Song has been a tremendously long one
As all us Brummagem's get our Brummie Day in the sun
By hosting a great Commonwealth Games. Oh what a lark!
It was so much more than a fifty kilometre walk in Sutton Park
Some serious sport is what the world's youth want
They came to Brum in their thousands to watch all us Brummagem's shine

Like the gems in The Jewellery Quarter. Oh what a place!
Where the gold medals, rings, necklaces & bracelets are made
And the Queen's baton too
96000 miles taken by a British Airways Crew to Cyprus the first point of frantic departure
We soaked it all in with a great opening ceremony
And dear old Brummie Bull stole the show and made the nations walk in harmony
As they marched round the magnificent new blue Alexander Stadium
With so many Brummie cars cavorting around the stadium
I think Sir Lenny Henry had had a tot of Jamaica rum
Let's hope we can be the destination of choice for the nation's great events like Eurovision
And show the world what we know that Brummies love to party down Broad Street
And dance the night away at the NEC and the Genting Arena
Brum's such a young City with so much creative talent to offer
And let all us Brummies see
Our great diverse City of Birmingham prosper

THREE LIONS ON A CERT

Three Lions on a Cert
'Arry Kane's still dreamin'
Three Lions on a Cert?
Southgate's still a schemin'
Chielini pulled Saka's shirt

Nearly killed a Gooner dreamkid

No one told the tricky Eyeties to lie down 4 the Pride of
England's Lions
Giant Gian Luigi Bonnamassa
Saved from our 3 Wonderkids
Saka, Sancho & Rash Ford
Triumph's out of disastaaaargh
These kids'll come again
Of that I am sooo shuuuer
Three Lions on a shirt
57 more years of hurt????
Still England are awaiting!!!!

With thanks to the Black Country's Frank Skinner,
Londoner David Baddiel & Liverpool's Ian Broudie of the
Lightning Seeds
Come on England!

BEAUTY IS?

Beauty is in the eye of the beholder
Does it diminish as the eye gets older?
Is it a catwalk model, size ten or sixteen?
Or a holiday-camp teenager crowned pageant queen?

A thoroughbred horse
Or a Kennel Club hound?
Beauty like our faith
Is indeed all around

A faceted diamond
Or a late vintage wine
The food on a table
Set ready to dine

A clear coastal view
Or the prettiest flower
The image of beauty
Can change by the hour

A new born baby
Or a bright blushing bride
Looked at by a husband
With love and such pride

A beauty spot here
Or a fine freckle there
The glint of an eye
Or the colour of hair

With clear skin or wrinkles
As a face gets older
Beauty indeed
Is in the eye of the beholder

BRUMMAGEM'S SONG

If you've never been to Birmingham then you ought ta
It's a grand city made up of many a quarter
There is jewellery to be sold, diamonds, platinum and gold
Boulton's silver to assay, precious gems from far away.
Guns were made nearby, helping soldiers fight and die
In the English Civil War, we made musket, cannon and ball
A more powerful Lewis gun helped the British beat the Hun.
Mr Webley made a revolver fired by many a pitiful soldier
On a lighter note in The Theatre Quarter
The stage is set for talented daughters
The Rep, the Alex and Hippodrome
Encourage performers to make Birmingham their own
Chaplin, Burton and Olivier
Travelled here to perform their plays
Musicals, ballets and pantomime
Ensure cultural visitors have a good time
The NEC and NIA have changed their names along the way
The Good Food Show, Crufts and fashion galore
Ensure our visitors come back for more
In the Symphony Hall there was often a battle
Between the CBSO and Sir Simon Rattle
The Chinese Quarter is colourful and bright
A fantastic place to go out at night
Stir-fried noodles, a tantalising odour
A grand Dragon Parade from Wing Yip's Pagoda.
The Balti Belt, full of saris and spices
Tasty Asian food cooked with different rices
An area to visit to sample a curry,
At Adil's or Imran's there's no need to hurry
Bring your own beer, share various starters
Poppadums, Pakoras, Aloo with tomatoes

A 'curry in a bucket' naan size of a table
Mild, medium or hot, eat it all, if you're able.
Our City has Cadbury, Jaguar Land Rover too,
Speedway, rugby, and cricket for you
A passion for sport, you can hear the roar
For a goal scored by Blues or Villa football.
Indoor and outdoor, The Bull Ring Markets
Sell everything from cheese to carpets
The Germans come at Christmas time
Bringing Bratwurst, Schnitzel and Gluhwein
Birmingham has 'More Canals than Venice'
We also invented the game of lawn tennis.
The Botanical Gardens and Cannon Hill Park
Have flowers and lawns, hosting shows: 'What a lark!'
An airport, coach and New Street Station
Make us the "Centre of our Nation"
To travel by car to any function
You may have to negotiate Spaghetti Junction
The 'Stroll from St Philip's to St Paul's'
Where Boulton and Watt occupied the pew stalls
Pugin's St Chad's, the Roman Catholic Cathedral
Anglican St Martin's, on the steps to the bronze Bull
The Kennedy Memorial near Digbeth's Custard Factory,
Healed the wounds of the Irish after the Birmingham
atrocity
The Rotunda stood proud, tall and round
Blown to pieces with 'The Tavern in the Town.'
The City recovered, no flags at half mast
Brummies look FORWARD, don't dwell on the past
Our mixture of cultures live well together
Our heritage, our history will go on forever.

GOLDEN RINGS FROM THE JEWELLERY QUARTER

The Birmingham Jewellery Quarter
Is present in our Home
Enclosed in the engagement ring
I am pleased to call my own.
Twelve diamonds round a ruby,
Lovingly set ingGold
Handmade by excellent craftsmen
To wear till I grow old
Hannah Hill from Dodd & Co
Watched our love flourish and grow
This beautiful ring she designed for us
For a proposal made with minimal fuss,
Two circles of gold followed soon after
Made by her brilliant jewellery crafter
After twenty five years of married life
These rings bind us together as man and wife

THE BATTLE OF BIRMINGHAM

Brum is burning, Brum is burning
Fire.....Fire......Fire.....Fire
Charles Prince Rupert
Was marauding
Throughout the own
Throughout the town

Brum was Roundhead
Not for Royalists
Ride them down
Ride them down

Rupert killed them
Torched their houses
For supporting
Parliament
Not the Crown
Many murdered
Many murdered

By Rupert's Cavalry
Cut them down
Yet at Shireland
Was a Skirmish
Where Earl Denbigh
Met his end
Shot him down
Shot him down

No Justice
No Justice
For Brummagem
For Brummagem
Brum is burning
Brum is burning

Fire....Fire.....Fire...Fire
Battle's over
Battle's over
Poor Birmingham
Poor Birmingham

SOUTHSIDE JOHNNIES AND CHINATOWN JINKS

Down 'Olloway 'Ed
To Wing Yip's Pagoda
Leading the way
To Chinatown's lovely odour
A tasty meal cooked in a wok
At Chung Ying Garden
We're 'Ready to Rock'!
Ming Moon Buffet
All you can eat
As you stroll down the sidewalk
To Brummagem's Beat!
The Fox, The Hip
The Back to Backs
All open their doors to
Johnnies in Slacks
Southside's Silver Rhino
Surveys...... all she can see
From the slate grey roofs above
The many theatre-goers with glee!
David Bintley's Royal Ballet

Formerly Sadler's Wells
Puts on 'The Nutcracker'
For many well-heeled swells
Every Christmas
David's 'Glittering Show'
Adorns Chinatown
With lots of fake snow!
The young bucks from Elmhurst School for Dance
Apprentice lithe dancers preen and prance
The Hip's huge stage
The largest in the land
Welcomes the UK's biggest pantomime
And plays, musicals and bands
That adorn Chinatown

On 'Golden Pond'
Stir-Fried Noodles
And chicken feet
Fed to me by Miss Chan
What a fantastic feat!
To attract the Chinese
To assemble MG's
At Longbridge
Premier Wen Jiao Bao
He came to Brum

In Twenty Eleven to visit the Chinamen
After MG Rover went 'belly-up'
In Twenty Oh Six.......
Mike Whitby and Dutton
This 'marvellous man'
'Mister Birmingham Development'
Such a sad loss
As Clive Dutton reported to Mike Whitby: 'The Boss'
They launched Brum's 'Big City Plan'
In Shanghai, near 'The Bund'
Hoping to attract Chinese Yuan
To invest in England

To build MG's in our land, once again!
To save the jobs of many a Brummie man
In October Twenty Fifteen
Another Chinese premier came
Li Xing Ping was his name
This time Georgie Osborne took 'ilm ooooop North
No visit to Longbridge
This Time for 'The Man'
For Brum, that wasn't quite in 'The Big City Plan'
I recall in Twenty Ten on Adrian Goldberg's Radio WM
Show
Talking with Paul Kehoe of BHX 'Fame' about
Birmingham's 'Twin City' of Guangzhou

About 'Marketing Birmingham' to the Chinese
Using 'Dear Old Bill Shakespeare' whom the Chinese love
As they fly high into Brummagem
High 'Up Above'
Using Whitby's new runway
To come to the region
The Chinese love William Shakespeare
His Chinese fans are so 'Legion'
This Brummie Bard
"The Greatest West Midlander"
Has the 'power to attract'
More Investment to 'Brummagem'!

Paul Kehoe poo-pooed mine and Ducker's idea
But in Twenty Fourteen
It became clear
A 'No-Brainer' for 'BILL' to Market Birmingham to the
Chinese
More money for Brum!
Done it! With ease
NI HAO from this Brummie
XIE XIE on our lips
Welcomes Chinese to our supermarkets
Wonderful WING YIPS!
This 'Man of Fujian'
Came to Brum in The Fifties
Made it His home
Brum's Chinese so 'Thrifty'
So it is 'ZAIJIAN' from me,
The new Brummie Bard

HEY! Paul Kehoe;
It wasn't So hard
To market 'Dear Birmingham'
To the Chinese
Using 'Bill Shakespeare'
What a man from these Shires

The World's greatest playwright
A "Man for all seasons"
Our "biggest attraction"
For so many reasons
As 'Bill's' plays are about
Our common humanity
Macbeth's 'Vain Death'
And Lear's 'Huge Vanity'
The players do 'Strut the World's Stage'
In Stratford Town
Just twenty five miles
From Chinatown

BALTI BELT N BRACEYS

Ladypool Road or Stoney Lane
No two curries are the same
Sizzling Tandoori, Tikka too
Balti 'buckets' or Vindaloo
Kashmiri spices, herbs and veg
Chapatis, roti or naan bread
Adil, Imran's, where will you go?
It's the 'Taste of Birmingham' you know
The colourful shops in vibrant streets
Window displays of cut-up sweets
Silky saris, Shalwaar Kameez
Bags and jewellery that will please
Wedding venues for love's celebration
Attended by guests from everynNation
For flavours tasted and beautiful odours smelt
I've often visited Birmingham's Balti Belt

BRUMMAGEM'S BANDS

Birmingham has produced the biggest bands
With fabulous songs and adoring fans
Famous in Europe and the USA
Outstanding music here to stay
Rock from Black Sabbath and Judas Priest
Was heavy and loud, to say the least
The Move had 'Flowers in the Rain'
First record on Radio One so they claim
Dexy's sang: 'Come on Eileen'
The Dance Floor Anthem for Love's Young Dream
UB40 had a kitchen with a rat
While Sabbath's Ozzy bit the head off a bat
The dutchie was passed by Musical Youth
Duran Duran: 'Hungry Like the Wolf'
Led Zeppelin climbed a 'Stairway to Heaven'
The world's greatest band in '77
Electric Lights inspired Jeff Lynne
Moody Blues Knights in White Satin
Would Christmas be the same without Wizzard and
Slade
Performing the music Midlands' bands made!

BIRMINGHAM: THE UNIVERSITY OF LIFE

Back in Nineteen Seventy Six
When the hot sun baked the broiling bricks
And Denis Howell MP for Small Heath
Was 'Minister for Drought' in the searing heat
He urged us all to bathe together
And not run round 'Hell for Leather'
I went from Birmingham Grammar School Boy
To the University in Edgbaston with unbridled joy
This bright but callow Brummie lad
Became a Birmingham undergrad
Studying B.Com in the Muirhead Tower
Where the Paternoster Lifts ran hour after hour
Perpetual motion taking 'Tortured Souls'
To jump off this Brutalist Muirhead coil
When exams in accounts became too much to toil
Doctor Peter Cain my ancient tutor
Urged this fresh man to use the first punch-card
computer
This student donned a great coat and scarf
And would do anything for a 'Belly Laugh'
Like read the communist manifesto
At Peter Cain's educated behest, Oh!
Marx and Engels to the fore

As all us students fought 'The Class War'!
David Lodge's 'nice work' if you can gerrit?
Made university life seem so decrepit
To study accounts was my forte
Or so I often thought. Eh ?
But when the doubts began to creep in
And my 'number blindness' started to seep in
To my youthful callow consciousness
With such dire unfortunate consequences
My exam time worry started to show
And I was struck such a mortal blow

When I failed my exams in statistics and maths
But tutor Cain set me on a different path
To study law and forget the math
Peter told me I still had a bright future
No longer for me the statistical torture!
For this rugby-playing muddied oaf
On the Bournbrook pitches.... I used my loaf
And played for the university first fifteen
As an eighteen year old flyaway flanker
I made my debut for my Alma Mater
Where my rugby defined me as a young man
Without any sort of discernible plan
The first fifteen I played in October '76

Before I even made my debut for The Old Dix!
Julia Honeychurch was my squeeze
Back in Strathcona we 'Shot the Breeze'!
Mick's Café's Race and Carnival
Was what defined me as a pal
A 'Belly-Buster Breakfast' and a pint of Guinness
The aim not to throw up at the breathless finish
A two mile run from the student's union
Down to Heeley Road and a date with oblivion
Where bacon and egg were downed with glee
Before running back to 'The Mermaid in The See'
That's when it all went 'Pete Tong' for me
As I threw up and my salad days
Became carrots and peas
And I was in an alcoholic daze
While on my knees
All good fun to raise 'Cash for Carnival'
I was no longer a 'Freshman Virgin' in High Hall....!!!!!

BEARWOOD TOWN

I aye gunner leave 'ole Bearwood Town
I aye gunner leave 'ole Bearwood Town
I aye gunner leave 'ole Bearwood Town
Coz it aye tha sorta place ter gemme darn

Councillors Piper, Eling n Jaron
Do soo much fer are Bearwood Mon
Loike Billy Spake
Does fer thee 'ole Black Countray
Smerrick is Richard Marshall's patch
This local Councillor does Sooo Mutch
Fer Bearwood n Smerrick
Smethwick in a Stew n Lightwoods Park and House
Juss two of 'is projects. Ooh worra lark!
I, and others from 'is Bearwood Crew
 Did Volunteer
 Fer Smethwick in a Stew
 As a fantastic reward fer uz all
Who Volunteer fer are Bearwood
'N', What's more, we did volunteer

Fer tha Beer on tha Black Countray Buzz
Juss a few yers agoo the Sandon Road "SIX"
Did trundle too n fro
With thee 'Aglee Rowd crowd
From the 6 Terminus on Sandon Rowd, tha Buzz
Past Saint Chad's where I was barn
Way back in '58
Lookin' All ferlarn
As "A Babe in Arms"
I wuz taerken,'Ome
Ter live in a Flat
Above 67 ,Three Shires Oak Road.....
The chop suey bar
Chinese Food, made in 'eaven!

Me Mom n' Dad, Dot n Lez
Did scraerpe tergether enough cash
Ter raise a Deposit fer BRUM MUNICIPAL BANK
At the top of Willow Ave
It wuz their prank
Ter buoy an 'Owse
In Willow Ave
The first thee 'ad with an indoor lav
Me Bracey family
Did scrimp n save
Me Mom n Dad did werk sooo 'ard
Me Mom Dot at the Midland Red
In Rutland Road doin' overtime on a' addin' machine
Werkin' till she fell in ter 'er bed
Ter buoy this 'owse
They were soo brave tha Braceys!
Me Mom n Dad, tha Braceys lot Dot n Lez!

Apologies to South African Folk Singer Whistling Roger Whitaker and his 1970's Christmas hit: 'Durham Town': This is my Brum poem about my home town Bearwood

THAT'S ENTERTAINMENT
For 'Grand Designs' or 'The Motor Show'

Where in Birmingham does one go?
The NIA or NEC?
Look around: so much to see!
The Hippodrome for pantomime
The Alex for musicals with song and rhyme
Orchestral music at Symphony Hall
Or a play at The Rep, which is just next door!
For concerts performed after dark
Visit St Andrew's or Villa Park
Cultural events at Aston's Drum
Or Birmingham Royal Ballet for dance and fun
Art exhibitions at Birmingham Museum
Join long queues to go and see 'em
The magnificent organ in Hansom's Town Hall
Played for the 'Three Choirs Festival'
Venues to view, places to stay
Birmingham's the city to visit today!

THE STORY OF ADAM AND EVE

God made Adam from a 'handful of dirt',
Gave him animals to name......not to hurt,
Placed him in a garden that was paradise,
Adam said Eden was very nice,
The problem was......he was so alone,
So, God made Eve from his rib bone,
The couple loved God and did obey,
They listened hard when he had his say,
THE food in Eden is good to eat,
Everything is ripe, fresh and sweet,
THE fruit from that tree shows good and bad
IF you eat that fruit, it will make me mad,
Eve went walking in the garden one day,
When Satan, the serpent came and had his say,
The fruit from that tree will make you wise,
Try it and share some, he did advise,
Eve and Adam both ate the fruit,
Then realised they were in their birthday suit,

When God called, they were so ashamed,
Eve and the serpent were both blamed,
God was sad and gave HIS command,
From this paradise you both are banned.
Thistles and weeds will grow from the Earth,
Eve you will suffer, when you give birth.
Snakes and humans will always fight,
feet will stamp and fangs will bite,
Adam and Eve were banished to their fate,
God placed angels to guard Eden's gate,
Not allowed to forget what they had done,
The couple worked hard and had two sons,
A farmer called Cain and his brother Abel,
But the lives of these two men is another sad fable

LAST WORD

Keith Bracey as a student at the University of Birmingham in 1978 was diagnosed as being bipolar, a hidden disability which has coloured all his life.

He would like to thank my wife Mary for her love and devotion and for putting up with him!

The royalties from this publication will go to the Bipolar UK as this mental health condition needs more research. Keith Bracey plays his part by subscribing to the Bipolar Disability Research Network (BDRN) at the University of Worcester and their "True Colours" email newsletter which has been enormously helpful in gauging his mood.

Printed in Great Britain
by Amazon